Survivors Beyond Babel

By the same author:

BANNERMAN
A FATAL CHARADE
THE ADORATION OF THE HANGED MAN

Survivors Beyond Babel

MARK ELLIS

SECKER & WARBURG
LONDON

First published in England 1979 by
Martin Secker & Warburg Limited
54 Poland Street, London W1V 3DF

SBN: 436 14488 3

Printed and bound in Great Britain by
Cox & Wyman Ltd,
London, Fakenham and Reading

He'd been within the grounds of Rawley before, but this was the first time it had occurred to him to break into the house. It was odd, he told himself, that a single man and an old woman could live by themselves in such an open and unprotected place. It was difficult to imagine that they wouldn't feel threatened. He looked up at the front of the building, the long line of windows on the three floors, and the great doorway set so securely in the middle. Rawley. Decaying, even as he stood there on the gravel of the driveway. The mortar falling away from between the stones. The wood around the windows swollen with rot. The walls stained brown and green by damp and the algae that had gathered around the trickles from the broken drains. A part of history, as he might have been told at school. The thought amused him, and took him back the four or five years since he'd last sat in a classroom and listened. Rawley. A part of your past. One small but nevertheless very significant piece of your national heritage. A force in the industrial revolution, the Rosses, and a great family of administrators when India was struggling to escape from savagery.

Now Daniel Ross lived here alone, separated from his wife, alienated from his brother; an absurd figure, he thought, setting out on his daily pilgrimage to scrounge money for the various charities he worked for. He looked up, aware that there had been a change in the strength of the wind, for the large oaks that lined the driveway were restless.

On the second floor a curtain moved. Daniel Ross. Watching him.

He smiled, and wondered idly what action he would take. A confrontation here, on the gravel? He doubted it. Daniel Ross was helpless; a man middle-aged before his time, whose day-to-day existence was watched over by an old woman who had known him since his birth.

As if to challenge the figure behind the curtain, he set out across the lawn. Tall, his back bent slightly, his smile never leaving his face for a moment, he deliberately left the driveway where he'd parked his motorcycle and walked in a diagonal to the elm trees that lined the old coach track at the far end of the lawn.

An hour passed, and he moved freely about the now diminished estate. The Rosses had suffered, like so many other wealthy families, during the years since the last war, and he knew that much of the old acreage had been sold off. But greater change was to come. He stared sullenly at the building in front of him. Not that Daniel Ross would be the kind of man to understand that. There was a sturdy resilience about the man that would defy any knowledge of the future. He doubted that even force would make him understand.

The decision to break into the house surprised him, as there had been little but idleness behind his coming to Rawley. Yet once planted, the suggestion overwhelmed him.

He entered easily through the kitchen door and then moved without any hesitation across to the hallway. It was as though he had some right of access, he told himself, some guardian spirit which allowed him to move freely and without danger. Inside, the house was very much as he had expected. There was an emptiness about it, a suggestion of man's desire to build coupled with a very strong sense of his fear of failure. Yet it did not awe him, as he had thought it might. There was almost something of an anticlimax about walking through the house. At one stage he even thought of calling out. He felt capable of meeting any form of confrontation. Nothing mattered. Rawley might have belonged to the Rosses for almost two centuries, but at this moment it was his.

The feeling of exultation was shattered as he pushed open the door to the library. Whereas he felt that the atmosphere in those other parts of the house he'd seen was one almost of desolation, of a grandeur that had long since passed, the library had obviously been well maintained. He stood uneasily in the doorway, his jaw working ceaselessly, his eyes moving across the shelves of books, the desks and tables, and the latticed windows with their panes of stained glass depicting scenes from both the Old and New Testaments.

The force of the contrast between his earlier feeling of confidence and this present awareness of being genuinely awed infuriated him. He closed the door and stared out into the hallway. It was only then that he began to doubt what he was doing; he looked around nervously, worried that he had been seen.

As he stood there he returned to an image which had struck him as he had stepped inside the library. Daniel Ross, sitting quietly at his writing desk, with an open book in front of him. There was something wrong about this image. It was wrong that someone who had done so little with what he had learned should make such a show of the way in which he had gained his knowledge. There was a falseness about the room, about its comfort and its splendour, and it was this sense of falseness which he finally took away with him, and which allowed him to walk casually towards the front door.

Outside he wheeled his bike towards the main gates of the house. The silence suddenly overwhelmed him. The empty expanse of stone and brick, the open lawn, the almost unused and overgrown driveway, all appeared so alien and incapable of control that the feeling of awe he had experienced so recently in the library returned, except that this time he was aware also of fear.

Daniel liked to think that there was something permanent about Rawley. The old house. His father and mother. His grandparents. Generations of Rosses and the beliefs that they had upheld, their voices, their conversation, their liberal and, so Daniel liked to think, their somewhat eccentric attitudes, had left an indelible mark on the structure of the place. Rawley, he would expound, and with his hands in his pockets and his face turned towards the window and the lawns outside he used to think that his father would have been proud of the sentiment, Rawley represents something essentially English. What exactly he meant by this statement he either would not or could not say. Occasionally, an acquaintance would notice that Daniel Ross would generalise where others might have chosen to remain quiet, but then he was known for taking pride in his beliefs, his liberalism, his ability to understand the modern world with its fast pace and its raciness, while retaining at the same time a quiet preference for the more traditional way in which he had been brought up and which he still maintained. Let people find out about the world their own way, he'd say. Different generations have different ways of solving problems. It's not for us to interfere.

It was rarely noticed, however, that there were times when he seemed worried about life outside the stone walls of Rawley. Times when he would stare about him as if unable to understand what was going on; when he would find himself outside of a cinema in the West End, seemingly perplexed at the explicitness of the stills pinned to the boards; when, caught by a sudden bout of self-consciousness on a London street, he would stare down at the cloth of his suit, with its careful creases and its total respectability, and compare it uneasily with the clothes worn by those who passed by. For the most part, however, he was successful in repressing these moments of unease; they did not reflect the way in which he saw himself and he therefore saw no use in dwelling on them. Aberrations, he called them. Perhaps the result of a bad night, or something not quite properly digested. Everything, he would tell himself, had its place. Everything could be explained in rational terms if one only took the time. Football hooliganism. The National Front. The New Left. These were only transitory things; every age had its equivalents. The English had always had extremist movements – what about Cromwell's parliament, he'd ask? What about the Levellers? The thing, he'd say, the whole thing is to retain our ability to look at things reasonably. And looked at reasonably, from his own point of view at least, both Daniel Ross and Rawley had an important function in the complicated fabric of English society.

He'd awoken early. A bad start to the day. For some reason as he'd dressed and come down to breakfast he'd found himself thinking about the day six months ago when he handed over the last of the family properties, the bakery, to Johnathan Mortimer. A natural decision, and one he'd been urged to take by his financial advisers. But it had not been an easy thing. For years the Rosses had accumulated money, amassing it easily both in India and in the lightning growth of industrial England. In its heyday Rawley had hosted parties that were talked of in London. Rawley and Ross became two names that sounded well together, suggesting both comfort and wealth. But neither Daniel nor his father had inherited the ability to look after money. His father had been a quiet man who regretted intensely having been born into the twentieth and not the nineteenth century. His life had been lived enshrined by books and words; money had slipped through his fingers quickly, and Rawley began to show the signs of decay that were to become so obvious as Daniel had grown older.

There was, he knew, something shameful in signing that piece of paper in front of Mortimer. A sense of loss. A sense of having failed. A sense, more than anything else, of the future without a purpose. He absent-mindedly turned the pages of the morning paper as he ate his breakfast. From the corner of the dining-room Polly coughed into her hand and looked up. Mr Daniel was brooding again. Her face darkened. His wife, perhaps. It wouldn't surprise her. Or perhaps the tiles falling off the roof, or the water-pump breaking down for the second time that week. Or Abel. And she thought back to Daniel's younger brother and the years she'd spent over him after his mother died. Abel Ross. The two brothers alike as chalk and cheese. It surprised her the same blood ran in them both. It was Abel who was the clever one, she told herself as she watched Daniel fold the paper and put it down beside his toast. The machines he made. His trains as a young boy. His radios and all those other gadgets. But with Daniel Ross you had to send for an electrician to change a plug.

Polly was a local girl and had never been further than London in all her life. When her father, a small farmer near Horsham, had been forced to sell out just after the First War he had taken a job in a brickworks. There Polly had been born in an old converted gypsy caravan, a place which was to be her home until she came to Rawley at the age of fifteen. She had grown up singleminded and with no delusions about the very small area of the world with which she was familiar. In her early years she'd seen a number of women climb up her father's caravan steps and had shown no surprise when in turn each one of them packed up and left. Yet there was an innocence about her which these experiences appeared to have left untouched. Her world was composed of a mountain of half-truths, deliberate falsehoods, fantasies and extraordinary insights. It was peopled by elves, hobgoblins, angels, gentlemen, scoundrels, and sex maniacs. She believed that the sun was mysteriously moved around the sky by God Almighty and that the stars were the lights of Paradise. She would nod wisely when mention was made of London and call it that stinking tower of Babel full of devils and Chinese, and took it that men had but one object in life, which was to take unjust advantage of women. She saw shadows of men behind bushes in the evenings; she looked under her bed and stabbed wildly into closets and cupboards with broom handles before sleeping, and on Sundays she picked out salacious items from the papers and read them with her hands across her heart and her face flushed a deep red.

Towards Daniel and Abel Ross she felt none of this general hostility, though her feelings towards Daniel were tinged with despair. She watched helplessly as Rawley fell slowly apart and Daniel wandered through its corridors, slapping the stone-work and proudly telling guests that it would last another thousand years. Blindness, she'd tell herself, that was it. He couldn't see far enough to look after himself. Or his wife. He'd lost her too. She coughed again and moved across to the hatchway leading to the kitchen. Abel. He'd be thinking of Abel. Not that he'd ever really cared much for his brother; he wasn't going to fool her about that even though he'd come out and say, 'Polly, did Abel tell you when he'd come down next?' Which of course he hadn't, because Abel wasn't ever coming back to Rawley; he couldn't stand the place.

She too was worried. A couple of days earlier she'd seen one of Abel's friends standing outside the front door. She'd watched him from an upstairs window, waiting for him to press the doorbell. He hadn't; instead he had turned around, got on his motorbike and ridden off. She might have thought nothing further of the incident had she not woken up that morning to see him again with his face pressed tight against her bedroom window.

She weighed up the odds in her mind as she cleared the table. Perhaps the man wanted nothing at all. On the other hand, he had no right walking around other people's property like that. None whatsoever. Private property was private property, sacred, something that should be respected.

'I think you should know you've had a visitor, Mr Daniel. A friend of Abel's.'

Daniel looked up quickly. 'And what did he want? Did he have a message?'

'He didn't say anything.' When Polly explained what had happened Daniel found himself getting uneasily to his feet and wishing, almost aloud, that Julie were still with him. Julie had an instinctive capability for this sort of situation.

Yet he had let her go. Watched as she'd packed her bags that day, bustled out to the Triumph and waved goodbye. As he'd watched her drive off he'd told himself she was just going for a short trip. To Scotland, perhaps. Or to Paris. A couple of weeks at most and she'd be back. That had been three years ago.

He watched as Polly swept the crumbs off the table. Brisk. Efficient. That had always been Polly's way. She shut the door behind her and he recalled the figure he'd seen stroll across the front of the house the previous week. Fair-haired. Large. A slow gait as he ambled across the lawn. The eyes deeply set, the mouth pressed tightly shut as though frightened of what in a moment of carelessness might be said.

When he had seen the intruder for the first time Daniel had followed him closely from one of the upstairs windows. A hiker, he thought. Someone who'd lost his way. It was only when he'd seen the bike that he was sure it was one of Abel's friends. The motorbike had been placed just inside the main gates, but well within view of the upper two storeys of the house, and it was difficult not to think back to Abel and his mania for machines. Even as a young child Abel had pulled screwdrivers and pliers out of the nooks where they'd been hidden and applied himself with care and patience to the sockets and plugs around the house. As the years passed and Abel's knowledge and ability increased his hands seemed to grow vast and be constantly covered in grease. It was ridiculous, Daniel knew very well, to feel so disgusted by this element of untidiness in his brother but there was little he could do to hide it. As long as Abel continued to live at Rawley he produced a continuous stream of mechanical devices whose purpose he had early on not found it worth his time trying to explain. Abel, Daniel would say jocularly in front of company, is like a robot. He's programmed to do all kinds of marvellous things, but none of us mere mortals is programmed to understand what they are. Abel, for his part, would keep his face bent and say nothing. He was impervious to his brother's needling.

Daniel went to the window and looked out across the fields towards the woods. It would be the same young man that Polly had seen, he was sure of that. A friend of Abel's. But why not introduce himself?

He had never felt comfortable about Abel's friends. Not that he would ever have admitted as much in public, but in the privacy of his own home he would worry that Abel had fallen under the wrong influences. What, for example, made it so difficult for this young man to come up to the front door and knock, instead of snooping round the grounds like a vagrant? He'd been uneasy that first day he'd seen him, and he was uneasier about it now. Everyone had his rights to his own beliefs and his own way of doing things, so long as he didn't tread on other people's toes, but Daniel had found it impossible not to register a slight disquiet when Abel had started running around on motorcycles and showing no inclination to go to university. A life should be useful; even his father's life had been useful in so far as he had acted as a pillar of strength to the local community. And as indeed, he rationalised, his own life was useful. Ever since handing over the bakery his days contained a great deal of activity, driving throughout the country on the behalf of various charitable organisations. He knew that he was being used but he was content to be used. He was, after all, a face to present petitions, and an amusing after-dinner speaker at fund-raising gatherings. Every now and again he would question himself about this new role in life, but the answers were invariably the same. He gave what he had; he was a pawn, but a necessary pawn, nevertheless. People needed help and he was in a position to give it. He had no doubt that people belittled him and even made him out as something of a joke. But then, as he had said on more than one occasion, he would defy anyone to prove that he wasn't being of service, that he wasn't a useful member of society.

When Polly reappeared she swept past him and with a firm flick of her wrist settled a velvet cloth across the table. There was a grimness about the set of her face, however, which made him pause and ask, 'Something bothering you, Polly? If it's that fellow you were talking about then I shouldn't worry. Probably nothing at all.'

'The hospital phoned,' she said.

He watched her fumble with her dress. Perturbed. Outraged, perhaps. He felt half inclined to smile at the puritanism which underlay so much of Polly's vision, but suppressed it as he reflected that he had never intended Polly to know. Abel was to her someone abused by circumstance; not the father of an unwanted child.

'You should have told me, Mr Daniel. The poor thing.'

'She's perfectly all right, Polly. I put the girl in good hands.'

'Oh, it's not that slut I'm worried about. I'm thinking about your poor brother, led along by that hussy so he hardly knew what foot to put forward next.'

He continued to watch her as she found work for her hands. A vase to polish on her apron. A brass ashtray to take across to the hatch.

'What did they say?' he asked, attempting to sound casual.

'A boy.' She pursed her lips, rubbed her hands down the side of her apron and then strode across to the door. There she stopped and turned to say, 'I would have thought you would have confided in me, Mr Daniel.'

About Helga? Daniel had only met her occasionally, having generally shied away from contact. The idea that this girl was to be the mother of his own brother's child confused him. His reactions were so awesome that they threatened to raise yet more questions to which he was sure he had no answer. On the one hand he wanted to be able to accept Helga and the child; he wanted to be able to accept the situation and react to it unemotionally, to treat it as a natural event that called for no comment. On the other hand he was outraged. Marriage was sacred, not to be anticipated by children playing with feelings they could not handle. He did not see himself as a religious man, but he could not resist the conclusion that Abel had sinned.

The doorway was empty. Polly had fled, presumably to nurse her feelings in her own rooms at the back of the house. He went out into the hallway and hovered uncertainly around the telephone. He'd done the only possible thing. Abel had disappeared and so he'd taken it on himself to look after the girl and the child. But that didn't mean that he condoned the situation. He'd arranged for the girl to enter the nursing home because it had been his duty to do so. He'd even come round to the idea of accepting Helga as a cause; someone who needed his assistance, and whom through family obligation he was bound to help.

He was drawn very quickly away from thinking about Helga by a sense of uneasiness. Something unusual had happened. The pace of the house had altered. Without moving his feet he swung round slowly, taking in the main staircase, the passage that led through to the kitchen, the archway behind him through which he'd just come from the dining-room, and finally the door to the library on the far side of the hall, a door which he now noticed was open, when by all rights it should have been closed.

The sight of the young man sitting at his own writing desk, his jeans soiled from the dirt outside and his knee-length leather boots still wet and filthy from the mud, enraged him. 'What in the hell are you doing?' he asked. At the same time he looked around quickly for signs of damage. His eyes took in the complete sets of Dickens, Trollope, Eliot and Austen which he'd inherited from his father, the eighteenth-century novels which George Hutchinson, his father's long-time friend, had left him, and finally his own collection of books which he'd so painstakingly built up over the years, gleaned from shops in the Charing Cross Road and as far afield as Cambridge, Oxford and even Edinburgh. His library. The very centre of the house.

'You've no right. None whatsoever,' he continued.

His eyes settled on the book in the man's hand.

'What've you got there?' he asked. He made a movement towards the intruder, but stopped still when he realised that he was at a loss as what to do next. The young man continued to remain silent, though he did toss the book down on the desk. The title remained hidden, and though he tried Daniel failed to recognise it from the binding. 'What do you want?' Daniel asked next. 'Don't you think you owe me an explanation, snooping round the place and then coming in without permission?'

'I did knock.' The voice surprised him. It was quiet, a little sullen, but educated. Daniel looked again at the face. It was less heavy than he'd remembered, but there was an evasiveness about it; the eyes were kept turned away and the mouth was tightly drawn.

'Then you had no right to enter until you were asked.'

For a moment the eyes met his own; they were a surprising blue, and there was the discomforting suggestion of a smile.

'Or perhaps you don't respect the idea of private property,' Daniel continued.

The smile did not vanish, although the face continued to be turned partially away. More than he had thought possible Daniel found the young man's silence disturbing. A confrontation he could have handled, but this obstinate refusal to recognise what he was saying left him uncertain of what to do next.

'I know who you are,' Daniel said as he walked across to the window. It was spring. He looked at the lawn outside the library window. Then more quietly he asked, 'Where is Abel?'

The reply seemed insolent. 'Do you care?'

'Of course I care.' He turned about and stood with his back to the window. 'Is that why you're here? Do you know what's happened to him?' Daniel paced across the room, his confusion at the barrier between himself and the other person making him wish that he'd never come into the library at all. The fellow was probably harmless. Disturbed. Perhaps he needed help. 'If it's about Abel, then please tell me. You're his friend, I know that. I've seen you before. If he's in trouble then tell me and I'm sure something can be worked out.'

The chair by the writing desk was gently eased back and the young man rose to his feet. He was taller than he'd seemed when sitting down, but thin, and his hands long-fingered and hanging limply by the side of his jacket.

'You like helping people, Mr Ross.' It was neither statement nor question, and, lost uneasily between the two, appeared thrown up as a challenge, almost with derision.

'If I can. Naturally.'

'How? With these?' The long fingers played quickly down the backs of a row of books. As he caught Daniel eyeing him nervously, he added, 'Don't worry about me. I washed my hands. They're clean. See?' He held them up, palms outwards.

Daniel stared at the hands, then reflected on the comment. Yes, books did mean a lot to him. Words. Words had formed his father's world, reached out to gather in a small group of closely knit friends, then closed in and buried him for all his sixty years till he'd finally died that night in front of the television. His father's world. His own too. They had taught him about the past, not just the ancient past of Rome and Greece and other even earlier civilisations but about his own more immediate English past. His Englishness and his place in the country had been understood through books and the knowledge they'd given him. Words were the beginning and the end; outside their tight framework lay chaos. This young man knew enough to challenge him. 'With these?' he'd said, and touched the books, as if to mock him.

'I think you should tell me what you want. You don't break into people's homes without having some intention.'

'I didn't break in.'

'No one let you in.'

'The back door was open.'

'But you still had no right.'

'Then call the police.'

'Don't be absurd. Is it about Abel?'

'I want to know about Helga.'

The simplicity of the request surprised him. Helga. Of course he would know her too.

'Has she had the baby?'

Daniel nodded.

'Where is she?'

Sensing that he had reached a bargaining ground Daniel said, 'Not till you tell me about Abel.'

The eyes met his and the smile returned.

'I don't see that there's anything funny in any of this. A young girl and an unwanted child. Do you think that amusing?'

'I was thinking of you.'

'Good God, your impudence is beyond belief.'

'I was wondering why you'd decided to look after her.'

'Someone had to.'

'I thought we lived in a Welfare State. She'd have been taken care of all right.' The face was turned away and the hands reached out for a book on one of the shelves. Daniel could see the title clearly this time. *A Room Of One's Own.* His mother's book. A gift to him just before she died. It had lain around the house a long time, he recalled, and for years he'd thought of it as nothing more than a guide to home decorating.

'Will you please replace that book.'

An attempt was made to replace the book on the shelf, but in the process it fell, scattering half a dozen pages across the carpeted floor.

Daniel strode across to the fallen book and snatched at the pages. 'I think you've done enough damage,' he said. As he stood up with the book in his hand he noticed that the smile had left the man's face and that now the cheeks seemed more flushed.

'I want to know where she is.'

'And I don't see that it's any of your business. Now get out.'

'I'm sorry about the book, Mr Ross. It was an accident.' The voice died away, then almost as though he regretted the apology he added, 'Still, what does it matter? You've got enough, haven't you?'

Daniel pretended to ignore him, but nevertheless watched closely as he walked out of the library, strode across the hallway and let himself out of the front door.

He watched the baby with the same reserve with which at a much earlier age he had observed the lizards and slow-worms that Abel had kept in glass cages not so very dissimilar to this present incubator. Daniel had never properly adjusted to his younger brother's affection for reptiles any more than he had ever really properly adjusted to so many of his other passions. But then for Abel the world was for a long time filled with an endless spread of accidental delights amongst which he moved without any other purpose than that of pleasure.

As he stared into the incubator, Daniel remembered the dry sand and dry skin of Abel's reptiles. The child fascinated him. A part of his own inheritance; and in the absence of his own children, he thought grimly, his sole link with the future. How long he stood there outside the nursery window and stared in at the naked, still half blue body with its thin face and bulging eyelids he was not sure, but he was aware of other people coming and going and that on several occasions a nurse would come and watch him from the doorway. Of course, he thought with embarrassment, they all thought it was his child. Who else, but a slightly dazed and overwhelmed father, would stand and stare so long at an infant at which no one else would have given more than a clinical glance, an infant in fact which was barely alive and stood only an even chance of outliving its new-born ugliness?

'Mr Ross?'

His name, declaimed so clearly and with such authority, made him turn round quickly. The nurse was smiling, which he was certain was an attempt to reassure him. In fact, it put him even more on his guard. Helga, after all, was only seventeen while he looked every day of his thirty-six years.

'I'm sure you'd like to see your wife, Mr Ross.'

'She's not my wife.' He realised that his mouth was dry. 'My brother's,' he added, though the words were barely audible.

'You have a lovely boy, Mr Ross. I'm sure you're thrilled.'

There was something purposeful about her that would not be dismissed. Together, silent and for his part very wary, they set off towards Helga's room.

'Look,' he tried, as they stood outside the door, 'there's something I want to get sorted out . . .'

'She's still a little tired,' the nurse cut in, opening the door and indicating that he might enter.

He found Helga lying propped up against the pillows. She seemed remarkably fresh, almost indecently so, he thought, compared to his own restlessness.

'Have you seen him?' she asked immediately.

He had not known what to expect from her, largely because he had been so preoccupied by his own role in the affair. And yet undoubtedly Helga was the main participant and he was glad to have his own concerns matched by hers.

'I don't know much about babies,' he said, 'but he looks fine enough. He's got everything he should have. Won't they let you see him?'

She shook her head. 'Not yet.'

Helga was a child. A beautiful child with messed hair and pallid cheeks. As he stood beside the bed he thought of the two together. Abel and Helga. The names kept going through his head until it occurred to him that there was now another one. Nameless. A child for the children. Abel, after all, was only nineteen.

His uneasiness remained as it struck him that he had no idea what to say to her. A joke, perhaps? He wondered if he should say something about the hair on the baby's face but thought that perhaps it might worry her. Of course the Ainus of Japan were hairy, but that would be small consolation. He should have brought her flowers. If that damned boy hadn't upset him so much that morning then he'd have remembered. He reminded himself to ask Helga about him.

'All this,' she said, looking round the room. 'It must have cost you a bomb.'

'Oh, I can afford it,' he laughed, pleased to feel on firmer ground.

'Abel said you think a lot about money.' It was said in innocence. He was sure she couldn't know that she had hurt him. And it was unfair of Abel, although Abel often didn't mean what he said. Words fell away from him with careless abandon. They had no more significance than the stars; things to be enjoyed, but ultimately beyond one's control. At the same time he recognised that Helga was brave. She could talk of Abel, while he had not even known how he was going to introduce his name. The bare truth was that Abel had run away; she probably wouldn't see him again. The child was an accident. He envied her courage; he was moved by her blindness.

As he sat down on the bed beside her he realised there was a face in the doorway. They were being watched.

'They don't understand,' he said. He silently cursed the nurses and the hospital. He even cast a momentary curse in the direction of the infant in the nursery.

Helga looked at him without comprehension.

He was tired. He had hardly slept for two days, worrying about Abel, about his wife, whether he would get Helga to the hospital in time, worrying even about his own future. His nerves were in pieces.

'They think I'm your husband,' he whispered.

She laughed, then surprised him by kissing him firmly on the lips. Out of the corner of his eye he saw the movement in the doorway.

'I like you,' she said.

'You remind me of my wife,' he said, without thinking. He was going out of his head. What he really needed was a couple of days rest in the hospital himself. 'I should have brought some fruit,' he said next.

'I'm going to call him after you,' she said. 'Daniel.'

His grandfather would have been pleased. The old man had died still virile and lecherous in his seventy-fifth year, with the words of the Old Testament spilling out of his mouth right until the final cackle had caught him as he had launched into Ecclesiastes, the preacher.

'The Lord loved Daniel,' he said helplessly. Dear God, perhaps Julie had been right after all. Daniel, can't you stop yourself, just for once? Can't you stop trying to describe things and instead relax for a while? The image of Julie in a flowing nightdress yelling at him from the top of the stairs disturbed the austere geometry of Helga's private room. Delilah. Judith. The good book was full of the deeds of foul women.

'Helga, there's some things I've got to straighten out. Abel, for a start.'

'I don't know where he is.'

She'd sunk back on the pillow. Tired, he could see that now. She shook her head to emphasise the denial.

'But he's the father. Why isn't he here?'

'What would he do here?' Her eyes seemed suddenly much older. Her question disturbed him. She obviously lived in her own world, and incredibly it appeared to exclude Abel.

'You'll need money. You think it's going to be fun out there trying to raise the boy on your own? And Abel . . . I'm worried about him.'

It struck him then that they both knew. Both Helga and the young man he'd come across in the library. 'I don't know,' he said wearily. 'I don't know why.' But he couldn't explain. He had dreams of Abel as the victim of men whom he couldn't see. Daniel the prophet.

Helga was looking at him, and he wondered if it was not with pity. After all, who was he to talk? What kind of example was he when all Helga had to do was refer to his own disastrous marriage with Julie? She took his hand and squeezed it. It was a measure of how far apart they were, he realised, that he wondered how he should respond. The touch of her hand embarrassed him.

'Does he look funny?' she asked.

'He's bluish, but he'll get over it.'

'Does he look like Abel?'

Abel had glasses as thick as rocks in front of his eyes. His hair grew like gorse over his head. He slouched. He had kept lizards as a young boy and then spent much of his adolescence having fantasies about acting in blue movies in Los Angeles. 'Like Abel?' He remembered that the infant had a tube sticking into its body, though where exactly he could not recall. Dear God, what if it didn't make it? He prayed briefly, then saw Jehovah glaring down at him and bellowing in anger at his impertinence.

He forgot to answer her as his own preoccupations took over. 'Helga, I'm going to have to ask you some direct questions,' he said. But even before he had started he knew that he had lost. She spun a lonely isolated orbit of her own making, and her child was nothing but a tiny planet sucked out of her body and destined for a time to revolve helplessly about her. She and Abel were a pair. Essentially isolated bodies that had crossed in time by accident. It was a philosophy which he could not accept; it defied his own definitions of reality. He could never get through to her, any more than he had ever made any real contact with Abel. Troilus and Cressida, Heloise and Abelard, even David and Jonathan – these were the pairs that belonged to the basic tradition which had moulded him. Helga and Abel were part of something new. Something he could not define. An alien system whose relationships were beyond his understanding, perhaps even his perception. The old order was not perhaps quite dead, but it was definitely dying. His attitudes, traditions, the mythologies which formed his points of contact with past and present, were all about to be overthrown. His ridiculous pursuit of his wife, his sentimental attachment to the days of Empire, even this desire he had to communicate his knowledge and feelings to the younger generation were all indications of a man whose world was in transit, and for whom the future held nothing certain at all.

'Do you think that if anything had happened to Abel then one of his friends might try to tell me? Does he have any friends who would do that, Helga?'

'Nobody wants to hurt Abel. He's harmless.'

'Someone did come to Rawley, Helga.' He described the morning's visitor briefly, adding that he'd also been seen around the house a day or two before.

'So Edgar did go to see you,' she said. There was a note of surprise in her voice, and beneath it a suggestion of delight.

'You know him?'

'Oh, Edgar was always getting at Abel about you.'

'Why?'

'Nothing. He's nothing to worry about.'

Daniel attempted to picture the kind of conversation she was referring to. It disturbed him that anyone might want to ridicule his way of life without knowing anything about it; it struck him as mean and ignorant, and tainted with viciousness. It hurt him too to think that Abel had found it so easy to bring up his name in conversation; a man was defenceless in the hands of others, and there was rarely any dignity.

'He may be harmless, as you say, but I was puzzled by his behaviour. He wouldn't say why he came, except that he asked about you.'

She nodded, but said nothing.

'But he didn't say what he wanted. He never even tried to explain himself. Is he always like that?'

'Perhaps he was just curious,' she suggested. Then when Daniel looked at her blankly, she added, 'About you.'

He thought about that before saying, 'I hope you'll tell him I don't want him round at Rawley again.'

He felt her withdraw from him. She turned her face away and stared at the window.

Angered by her reaction he said, 'I think I have a right to know what he was doing there.'

'What rights do any of us have?' she demanded. 'Who asked me if I wanted to come to this place? No one. It was you, interfering as you've always interfered. We never wanted any of your bloody charity. I never heard Abel say that you asked him what he wanted to do with his life. It was always what you wanted him to do.'

She started sobbing. Within a few seconds her face had turned red and was blotched with black streaks. The sheets were crumpled in her fists and drawn up to her neck.

'Well, just remember that it was me who looked after you when you needed it, not Abel. Where in the hell is he when you need him, just tell me that?' He had visions of the door bursting open and the entire hospital staff coming in to find out what was going on. 'I'm sorry,' he said. 'That was unnecessary. I shouldn't have said it. The truth is that I'm tired. Tired and worried.'

He paced up and down the room, finally pulling a cigarette out of his pocket and setting it in the corner of his mouth. Obeying easily the years of training his mind cancelled out Helga and the hospital room while he fought the compulsion to light the cigarette.

She watched him stop and bring out a box of matches.

'Edgar always said that he'd pay you a visit,' she said.

Daniel turned to her.

'To see for himself. What you were like.'

'But why me?'

'He said you fascinated him.'

'I don't want him there again. Next time I'll have the police in.'

'He won't do anything.'

'That's beside the point.' Then what was the point? That he was frightened? But he had nothing to be frightened about. Perhaps the truth of the matter was that he should have let Abel go his own way and not interfered with his affairs at all. That way none of this would have happened.

'The point is,' she said, as though reading his mind, 'that you shouldn't have brought me here at all. It's only guilt, isn't it?'

The crudity of the comment astonished him.

'Because of her.'

He stiffened.

'You know who. Your wife. Your ex-bloody-wife.'

As though she had been watching from outside, and probably had been too, Daniel told himself later on, the nurse came in and within seconds was between them, fluffing up the pillows and rearranging the sheets.

'I expect Mrs Ross is very tired,' she said, smiling at him as she turned round.

He grunted, drained of energy and too weak even to make the protestation he'd so ineffectually attempted before.

At the door he turned and said, 'Helga?'

But she didn't look at him.

Daniel drove the twenty miles to Brighton in just under forty minutes, the small lanes that still pass for roads throughout much of Sussex taking him through countryside he had known since childhood. He registered little of the day except that the air was crisp and the light was sharp. April. Together with Julie he had walked the Downs many times at this time of the year, taking packed lunches and following paths and tracks which had existed for hundreds of years across the gently sloping contours of those harmless hills. It was impossible now for him to see the Downs without remembering Julie and his own past; impossible to see them without the awesomeness of knowing one was part of a heritage that stretched back to times so lost in myth that one could no longer see with any clarity at all. Through the Downs and into Brighton. A modern town, and yet with its own very singular hold on the past, with echoes of Regency and wrought-iron Victoriana intermingled with a modern Babel of tongues from throughout Europe and Asia; and beyond it the Channel, where with little effort he had often conjured up images of the Armada beating its way round to Dover and of the great clippers in later days on the way to the East and Australia. The same shoreline, chalk and pebbled beach. The same sea. The same winds. The present almost an illusion one might conveniently forget, a doorway opening back into the past, when forests still covered the Weald and crept up to the chalk of the Downs. Julie had at first laughed at what she called his ravings. He'd taken her to look for twayblades and early purple orchids in the first months of summer; to him they brought back childhood, but she picked them only to let them fall as litter five minutes later on.

Mrs Roach, Abel's landlady, greeted him profusely as always and dragged him in for a chat and a cup of tea before allowing him to go up to Abel's rooms at the top of the house.

'No letters, nothing,' she said, once he'd managed to steer himself out into the corridor. 'Who would have thought it? Such a considerate young man. Was always writing me postcards, Mr Ross, Abel was. Greece and France. Ever so thoughtful. When he was over there' – Mrs Roach always referred to America as 'over there' or 'that place' – 'he sent me a letter.'

Mrs Roach was one of the better influences in Abel's life; indulgent, open-hearted, blind to the faults of those she loved. She looked at Daniel critically. 'You look awful, Mr Ross. White. I couldn't see you properly in there, not without my glasses, but the light's a bit better here. You do look terrible. Whatever have you been up to?'

'Mrs Roach. About Abel. Did you notice anything before he left? Anything unusual?'

'Unusual? Well, there never was very much usual about Abel, was there? I mean someone else might think he was unusual all the time.'

'No, not like that. Anything that made you think things were not quite right.'

She touched his sleeve. They were standing out in the corridor. She was a small lady, slightly myopic, but with a very firm grip on life. Her house, left her by her brother, had provided income for her family over the past twenty years. It was a neat house and well kept. Her lodgers were lucky and tended to stay for a long time.

'You know, Mr Ross, I've never said anything to Abel. Never. I wouldn't think it right to do such a thing. But he's had me worried. Some of the people I've let in through that front door I wouldn't have let in for anyone but him. But then it's not always the same type. Had all types of friends, Abel did. I'm sorry he's caused you so much trouble, I really am. Still, his flat's just as it was when he left. I've tidied it a bit but I wouldn't know where to start if I was to clean it out.'

Abel's flat was pretty much as Daniel had last seen it. There was a lack of cohesion about it, a general abandon which described the state of chaos in which Abel appeared to exist. Yet Abel had rejected the verdict with a typical shrug of the shoulders.

'Chaos?' he'd queried, flopping down on the bed. 'There's no chaos. You can't see the order, that's the real point.'

Daniel looked at the bed and remembered Abel spread across it. How the boy had grown so thick in the body and neck was a wonder which he had never grown used to. The family was by nature and precedence tall and thin. The men for centuries had been disposed towards tuberculosis, a hacking cough and an early death; the women were generally anaemic, and lived for years into devastating senility. But Abel was an aberration. His body was bearlike, his neck like a short and muscular tuberous growth beneath his great woolly head. Only his legs gave any indication of his heredity. They were thin and bulged at the knees; characteristically, they were the only part of his body in which he'd shown any pride.

'Then what plans do you have?' Daniel had asked him. 'What do you intend doing?' The occasion had been Abel's rejection of the idea of university.

'Go back to America,' came the reply. 'Perhaps.'

'You hated it when you got there,' Daniel reminded him. 'It was just a dream you had. Something you invented.'

'People are always inventing America,' he answered. Abel had an annoying habit of being provocatively sententious at times. Usually Daniel could point out that in fact he was merely quoting or parodying someone else, but Abel would only laugh. 'Anyway,' he'd continued, 'I like it there. They think I'm normal.'

'And what about Helga? Some people might say that you're running away from your responsibilities.'

'Helga doesn't think that way.'

'But I do. And so would other people.'

'It's Helga who's having the baby,' he pointed out.

'She's a child, Abel. She doesn't know what she's thinking about most of the time. Her head's full of half understood logic, and . . . for God's sake, she just doesn't understand anything. She's got a child's perception of the world.'

'So what do you want to happen? That she should want me to marry her?'

'What about the child? You think it won't need a father?'

'Children get raised without fathers. I did.'

Impossible, they'd called Abel. His parents, before their death – and then he'd been no more than a toddler running around the few rooms they'd restricted themselves to after his birth. His teachers too had come to the same conclusion.

It was in his early adolescence that Abel had started to show the curious interest in America and things American which was later to grow into such an obsession. Where this came from Daniel didn't know and Abel himself could give no real reasons. What was indisputable was that the pattern had existed in a more unformed state since very early childhood when he showed more than average interest in Disney cartoons and Coca-Cola than the normal British child of his age. In those days Abel had an unnerving habit of slipping into faultless imitations of Donald Duck and Bugs Bunny, and even a spell in an expensive preparatory school did little to stabilise his use of language. While his peers at the age of nine and ten were capable of producing natural treble replicas of their parents' vowels and stress patterns, Abel developed a Cagney whine which he would accompany with a Bogart tilt of his school cap or a fast Gene Kelly stride on his pinstick legs. The boy's behaviour proved a source of both embarrassment and annoyance to the school authorities and it was not long before a letter reached Daniel, who was by that time guardian of his younger sibling, asking him to remove Abel from the school. After that initial proof of his singularity Abel never managed to remain long in any school. He saw himself as an anomaly, an acceptable if sometimes uncomfortable joke played on national boundaries by nature. By the time he was thirteen he had totally abandoned any claim to being British at all. He spoke with a perfect Brooklyn accent which never lost its characteristic nasality and long gliding whine, even when his voice broke. His rooms, because at that time he was still living with Daniel at Rawley, were a museum of junk and the flitting fads which caught his imagination. The walls were festooned with pin-ups of Clint Eastwood and Marlon Brando and, reflecting his more mechanical side, Ben Franklin and Edison. Centrefolds from *Playboy* overlapped scenes from Disneyland in such a way that it was difficult to see where one began and the other ended. Piles of *Life* magazine and *National Geographic* stood up in bound bundles on the floor. In one small room off his bedroom the Santa Fé railroad moved through papiermâche Rockies, dying Apaches, burning homesteads and the Fifth Cavalry at full gallop. The Statue of Liberty stood on the mantelpiece above the curiously English gas fire. A copy of the Declaration of Independence was nailed to the door. Daniel had watched him nail it there, and thought back to Luther at Wittenburg. Abel in Levis and workshirt, a twentieth-century iconoclast baring his teeth at his brother and everything his brother stood for, at everything the house, with its past set square in the days of Empire and its memories of past generations of Rosses, represented.

'Do you have to?' Daniel had asked him as he had banged the Declaration firmly into the door.

'Up your ass,' Abel had replied without a moment's hesitation.

Thirteen years old.

This present room told the same story, except that Abel was now nineteen years old, and incidentally a father. It was cold in the room, and Daniel stood there staring at the bed, his hands in his coat pockets, his thoughts drifting haphazardly, completely at the mercy of his senses.

One night Abel had gone on incoherently into the early hours of the morning about a long ride in a '53 Studebaker across six states, which had ended up at high tide at Newport Beach. Daniel had listened with fascination to what he could understand, but even so he could not satisfactorily imagine Abel at the age of sixteen in California. The truth was, of course, that he should never have let him go. Shamefully, Daniel found himself admitting that in some ways Abel was a product of his own incompetence.

Some five minutes later he started to go through Abel's possessions, at first going through drawers and frantically pulling out clothes that had obviously not been worn for years. Amid the old torn jeans and the endless T-shirts, the thick sweaters and the now useless school ties, he recognised a side to his brother which he had long forgotten. Abel was a hoarder. Although he had rarely shown any attachment to his possessions there was something in him which made him frightened of throwing anything away. The old clothes began to pile up on the floor around him; they stank of mildew and long-dried sweat. With them he pulled out torn copies of girlie magazines. Packets of condoms. A magazine with addresses and suggestive poses for swinging singles in the Los Angeles area. An old photograph of Abel as a child: his eyes had always been bad, his hair always unruly, his torso always thick though in this particular image it was merely rotund. Across the back his name was written in a barely identifiable childish scrawl. Abel. Abel. Abel. Daniel counted the name twelve times.

The rest of the small flat told him little that he did not know already. A cricket bat which had not been used for almost eight years was propped up in a dust filled corner. A school photograph was tacked to the flowered wallpaper just above the stereo. Record sleeves bearing the names of classical composers and modern pop idols were indiscriminately stained with coffee and other less identifiable substances. An old pen with its barrel still stained with long-dried ink lay against the skirting. In spite of all the casualness, Daniel was moved to think that his brother was so attached to the past. In a way, this apparent fear he had of separation from the objects he had accumulated over the years was the nearest their two quite separate systems had ever come to making contact.

It was only when he was just preparing to leave the room that he stumbled on something that caught his interest. The first clue was a photograph of Julie. That Abel had a crush on her, Julie and Daniel had accepted for years. As a young boy of twelve, just about the time when his voice was beginning to change and his face to show the first signs of a beard, Abel had taken to following her, not only around the house but outside in the street as well. Those were the days of Abel's first love letters: painful, illiterate meanderings, which were full of awkward suggestions about drive-in movies, clambakes, hot-rods, jive, jazz and other words which quite definitely at this age could have meant very little to him. Hundreds of those letters made their way from Abel's desk to his wastepaper basket, balled up and scoured by what looked like teeth marks. Julie had been openly amused by all this, but Daniel had been concerned.

'But he's so young, Daniel,' Julie had said. 'It's all perfectly innocent. To him, I'm pure. A sort of Virgin Mother thing. His Lady of the Rose.'

Julie never convinced him about that. Even in those days Daniel knew that Abel's eyes clouded at the mention of sex. He kept badly printed books and colour magazines from Germany under his pillow and mattress; Abel did not see anything pure in Julie, Daniel was quite sure about that.

The photograph of Julie was not one that he recognised. He thought that she could have been only about nineteen or twenty when it was taken as there was still that devastating freshness in her face which the marriage, he had to acknowledge, had so quickly taken care of. Where Abel had got the photograph he did not know, but it brought him up with a start. It was tucked under a book – Castaneda (Abel had once expressed a wish to go to Mexico and if possible die from an overdose of peyote) – and as he pulled it out there came with it a sheet of paper which bore writing he knew only too well.

The dateline at the top made him reach for the chair and sit down. January the eighteenth. Only three months before. He read quickly.

My dearest Abel,

You must not, absolutely must not, see Davison again. He really isn't any good for you, and frankly I can't imagine what you hope to gain from all those visits to his place. If he insists on seeing you then don't be frightened of using force. Bob might be older than you and somewhat overwhelming at times, but he's a physical coward. Please don't think I'm doing this just to interfere. I've always thought about you, Abel, however much it might have seemed otherwise.

Lovingly,
Julie.

PS. I send a photo. Recognise me? As you might have guessed, it is very much A.D. (avant Daniel).

PPS. Don't be frightened of asking Daniel for money to help

you and Helga. He's got pots of it and besides, half of it is rightfully yours.

The postscripts were typically Julie. Even after three years she still had the power to hurt. Daniel sat there mesmerised, staring stupidly at the photograph and wondering how he had ever let his life get so out of hand.

Aware that Julie's lifestyle had changed considerably since she had left him, Daniel was now able to admit that he had perhaps been a restricting influence on her – though he consoled himself by the thought that all marriages were restricting. Throughout their marriage Julie had always alleged that there were certain people who were basically terrified of life and needed someone else to draw in the boundaries for them, and Daniel knew that she had meant to include him among such people. Now that they were separated he used this as an argument to persuade himself that one day she would come back: he needed her, she herself had admitted it.

He knew her timetable as though it were his own. He knew her friends, her colleagues, her acquaintances. All her lovers – and Daniel was convinced that she had several, some younger and some older than himself – were catalogued in his mind. He knew them by profession, by age, by name. He carried pictures of them, sad young men with long hair, artists and solicitors, picked unsuspectingly out of a Saturday night crowd in Leicester Square, and he'd seen otherwise faithful husbands walk guiltily out of her doorway to return home to Epping and Ewell with placatory bundles of flowers and boxes of chocolates. He'd watched them all. He knew them all. He knew their wives and sisters, their children and their small front gardens. He carried visions of them into the upper rooms of Rawley; they entered his dreams at will and nodded as he called out their names.

Julie had always defied his definitions. A consultant engineer, she owned her own house just north of the river near Dolphin Square. Julie had money, part of it his, part of it her own. But what stood out most about Julie was that there was nothing consistent about her that he felt he could point to. He could see no matrix into which she readily fitted. She was an enigma.

However, after leaving Abel's flat in Brighton he had no other alternative than to try to persuade her to talk, and so during the afternoon he headed north on the A23 to London.

She opened the door while he was still gathering the courage to knock.

'Hullo, Daniel. Still snooping? I'd have thought you would have got tired of playing Sherlock Holmes in your spare time. Which,' and as if on cue she opened the door wider to let him in, 'you seem to have an increasing amount of these days.'

It had been nearly nine months since he had last been inside Julie's house and not unnaturally he had carried in his memory the rather dull if quite expensive interior which had seemed to characterise it. Now, it was all changed. The heavy furniture and the ancient carpets had been taken out. The embossed wallpaper had been removed. Daniel felt ill at ease in the lighter texture of these new surroundings – only an old grandfather clock which had originally come from Rawley remained as some kind of link with what had gone before. It was, he supposed, all typically Julie, with its thin-legged tables, the awful pop art prints, the imitation Bridget Riley, and yet at the same time it was rather aggressive in a cat-like way. The room was feline, and Julie sat curled on a small chaise-longue, smoking a cigarette and laughing. He felt that in some ways she had done it all out of spite – to defy his conclusions, to make him ill at ease.

'So what is it this time, Daniel? Or is it merely just a simple matter of prying into my private life yet again?'

'No, it's about Abel. I want to know about Abel.'

'Good heavens, darling, I thought you knew about Abel. You always seemed to have such strong views about him.'

'No, it's not that. I want to know where he is.'

She hesitated then. She put the cigarette down beside her and straightened her legs. As she faced him she touched her hair with one hand. He relaxed as he noticed a slight firmness set in about the mouth, an old habit of hers which had always indicated stress and perhaps uncertainty.

'Abel is your brother. Not mine.'

'I need help, Julie.'

She raised her eyebrows, then laughed. 'Good God, what's happened?'

'Abel has disappeared.'

'He's done it before. What makes you so worried this time?'

'You don't know where he is?'

'If I did I'd tell you. I haven't seen Abel for ages.'

'He hasn't written to you? He hasn't phoned?'

'Whatever for?'

'About anything. Anything at all.'

'This is all very mysterious, Daniel. Are you quite sure you're feeling all right? Or is it just that you're worried about having to give up the family pile? Though God knows, anyone who bought Rawley off you would be doing you a favour.'

He felt that the comment was calculated to hurt. She knew that he could not see himself as living apart from Rawley. The house was part of himself; it stretched back into the past and in many ways took him with it. He looked up at her nervously, and wondered if her smile was because she was pleased with what she had said. But then it was he himself who had told her about that morning in the Meerut room. Coronation day, nineteen hundred and fifty-three. His father's breakfast was always an important event, and that morning Daniel had shared it with him in the Meerut room, which was not much of a room at all, being more of a vast enclosed greenhouse whose glass walls and ceiling entombed many cubic metres of cloying humid air. The Meerut room had been named after Edward Ross, an uncle of his grandfather, who had died in that town during the Mutiny. Edward Ross had been a very quiet type, and, from his portrait which hung in the main hallway of the house, very similar in appearance to Daniel's father. Both men wore heavy sideburns and had about them that rare ability to stifle any attempt at joviality by those who came into contact with them. From all accounts Edward Ross had not been pleased to die. He had fought with uncommon aggressiveness for his life and had given it up only at great loss to the sepoys who had broken into his home. Daniel was later to know that his father saw an uncanny resemblance between himself and his ancestor, not only in looks but also in temperament. Edward Ross had become something of a legend in family history, and was held up as a fine example of still waters running very deep. He was, or at least his legendary figure was, the ideal apotheosis of the Arnoldian Victorian – a man steady in the path of Christ and not afraid of the truth. As they sat down together at the breakfast table Daniel had felt the presence of Edward Ross very strongly and was half inclined to excuse himself and go up to his room. The potted palms, the massive ferns, the trailing vines, the sticky wet air and the parrot that was kept chained in the corner all bore down heavily on him, and more than once when he looked across the table it was to stare into the features of Edward Ross, and not those of his father.

There were other reasons which made him associate this room with this early member of the Ross family. By all accounts, his own included, he was a great naturalist, and had spent months at a time trekking through the jungles of Assam and the foothills of the Himalayas in search of plants and insects. Even in those days – and he died before Darwin had published *The Origin of Species* – when man was unquestionably made in the image of God and an ape was nothing more nor less than an ape, Edward Ross wrote long monographs on the wisdom of the insects, the gentleness of plants, and the uncanny sensitivity of all living things to mood. Mercifully, these writings were never presented to a publisher but kept locked up by Sybil, his sister. Sybil, who'd died in that same room at Meerut, raped and finally opened up across a velvet upholstered chaise-longue, feared for the sanity of her brother, pleaded with him, begged with him to see reason – but he always insisted in his humourless fashion that he was right. Edward Ross spoke of singing to plants, talking to them, caressing them. His notebooks, which Daniel was to read at a much later date in the attic at Rawley, were a veritable erotica of strange pleasures. This much removed relation of his, quiet and outwardly morose that he was, Daniel was proud to realise belonged to the same mighty impetus that had produced the men of unlikely visions who had so transformed the landscape and imagination of Victorian Britain. Edward Ross had visions of strange auras surrounding all forms of life, of charges of energy constantly released into the atmosphere by living things, of all organic life belonging to a much greater whole, of a past that belonged to the future in as much as all cycles necessarily repeat themselves time and time again. Edward Ross saw the world as a place of many beginnings, not just one evolution but many. In so many ways he was a man born out of his time, and not, Daniel was sure, slightly unsound of mind, as Julie had so unkindly suggested.

The room, with its plants, the heavy air, evoked images of Meerut. As he sat there with his boiled egg neatly scalped in front of him, Daniel wondered if he was going to be sick.

'Important day, Dan,' his father had said. 'Fifty-three years and six of them I've seen. Victoria. Edward. George. Edward. And George again.' He paused a while before saying, 'You should study the first Elizabeth. I did.'

Daniel remained silent, mainly because he was used to pronouncements such as this and experience had taught him that they needed no additional comment. They were a form of reflection of his father's inner mind, of the constant ebb and flow of images that paraded through what he tended to imagine as the very gloomy corridors of his father's brain. It was what followed that made him sit up and listen.

'Glad to be home?' his father asked. The reference was to the permission he had obtained to come home from school for the Coronation.

'Yes. Of course.'

Daniel remembered himself as being dressed in his school trousers and shirt. The trousers were grey flannel. The shirt was white and open at the neck.

'What do you see ahead of yourself, Dan?'

The question hummed through his head for some time before he was forced to admit that he didn't know how to react. He hadn't understood what his father had meant.

'I'm talking about the future, you know. Might seem a bit strange, coming from me. But there we are; that's what I'm talking about. Your future. And in some ways that means the future of Rawley. What do you say, Dan?'

Daniel flushed red, looked up at his father and noticed that his eyes were set on his face, large brown eyes that were quite suddenly alive with enormous inquisitiveness and what much later he would have understood as humour.

'Perhaps you don't understand my question?'

'Yes, I understand it.'

'But do you know why I asked it?'

Daniel thought of the upper rooms slowly decaying. On his walks round the house he knew of further indications of decay: a water-pump that had broken down six months earlier and was still unrepaired, tiles were falling from the roof and were not being replaced, here and there the window panes were broken, and in the gutters the old nests left by the starlings had been swept into the corners of the drains.

'Of course, I'd like to be able to tell you that the house is going to be yours. Well, it might. But I doubt it. I'm not a very good man with money, Daniel. And the family has lost a lot of it over the years. It's up to you what you preserve. You'll have something left to you but if you want more then you'll have to fight for it.'

'Are you going to sell Rawley?' He'd found it difficult to understand what it was that his father was trying to tell him, but there did seem an awful possibility that Rawley might go.

'It would worry you, wouldn't it?'

'Yes, I'd hate it.'

He laughed. 'I believe you would.' He sat back and stared at his son. 'The fact is that in ten years' time we probably won't be able to afford Rawley. Unless something unforeseen happens the business will go bankrupt. The plant is old and we haven't the funds to replace it. If I live another fifteen years, or twenty years at the outside, then the chances are that I'll no longer be living here.'

He'd been stunned. He remembered that he'd squirmed in his seat and wanted to get away.

'I know you, Dan,' his father had said next. 'I know how much this place means to you, and I don't want you to be hurt. I don't want you to set too much store by Rawley. You ought to think ahead a little and broaden your horizons. Things are changing.'

'Rawley doesn't have to go,' he'd replied. 'It doesn't have to.' There'd been petulance in his voice, but there was fear also.

Daniel had always told himself that his relationship with his father had changed from that moment. Things were never again as natural as they had been. The days before were a golden age, mythical, beyond the necessity of accurate description. It was only from that moment that he felt he had actually begun to know fear and anxiety, and from those two to develop knowledge – the knowledge of himself that he was prepared to accept, and the knowledge of himself that he spent so much time trying to hide.

'That was an unkind comment, Julie,' he said quietly. 'You know I don't want to see Rawley go.'

He stared at the window. Outside it was just turning dark. Within fifteen minutes the lights would be on. The streets of London bathed in yellow light. And somewhere out there – Abel. She knew. She was lying.

'Still, you've had a good run,' Julie said. 'You and your father and all the rest of the family. All the Rosses living high on the hog for nearly a century. You should be grateful.'

'You're obviously not doing too badly yourself.'

'I dare say. But I work for it. You didn't do a damn thing for your money so you've little right to complain if things are bad for you now.'

'For God's sake, who said I was complaining?'

'Of course you are, Daniel. You're the gloomiest bloody man I've ever met. Your whole adult life has been nothing but a dirge for the end of capitalism and the leisured classes. Where would you be if your family hadn't gone to India and reaped the spoils of their unglorious rape?'

'It's not the money side of it. I can get used to the idea of being poor.'

'Don't be ridiculous. You'd die if you really had to earn a living.'

What he felt that Julie had never been able to understand was that it was not simply the money which he regretted, but the loss of an entire way of life. He consoled himself by thinking that Julie's world had always been quite different to his: a material world, full of things, money, objects with and without value.

Cause and effect she saw very much in financial terms. It was a simplistic view of life and under different influences, or had she ever bothered to read, then she might have become a radical socialist. It was, he supposed, because in a way hers was a very selfish world, devoid of love, and which it was easiest to describe as being the result of unavoidable material influences. Julie's father had fought for what he had and she had witnessed the battle, and counted the gains and losses as the years passed. What she could not see was that he regretted the end not just of the money, but of an entire age and the structures which that age had built. He regretted the inevitable loss of Rawley, the house the family had taken over one hundred and seventy years before; he regretted the loss of a landscape, given over to small estates with their awful levelling effect on the consciousness of those who lived in them; he regretted the gradual shattering of the past and the imposition of a present which did not belong to him; he regretted the lack of faith in words, the way in which they were manipulated so that instead of fostering human dignity they had become the agents of its abuse; but above all, he told himself, he regretted the loneliness that had resulted from losing her, his wife.

Julie and Abel. He couldn't bear to lose either one of them, yet it struck him then that in fact he had lost both. Julie was never going to come back. And Abel? Abel had already gone.

'I know you've seen Abel,' he said.

She laughed and got up.

'No, please listen,' he said, following her across the room.

'You'll have to go, Daniel. I'm expecting someone.'

He grabbed her by the arm. 'Who? Business?'

'Really, Daniel. Why should I have to answer?'

'Because I have to know.'

'A friend,' she replied. 'Now please let go of my arm.'

He released her but still followed her out of the room. At the bottom of the stairs she turned and said, 'Run along now. I'm asking you politely.'

'Where are you going?'

'Upstairs. To change.'

'For him?'

'Yes. If you must know.'

'Why did you lie about Abel?'
'I've no idea what you're talking about.'
'You wrote him a letter.'
'I did?'
'About Bob Davison.'
'Then don't ask me if you already know.'
'Are you going to tell me why you implied you hadn't written when you knew damn well that you had?'
She stared past him, then said, 'I'm going to change.'
'Where is he, Julie?'
'I've not the slightest idea. And why can't you leave him alone and let him run his own life? Can't you understand that people can exist without your constant interference?'
By this time Julie was halfway up the stairs. She stood defiantly against the banisters. Her hair, which had always been so magnificent when long, was cut short and ragged in comparison. Her clothes too – the stained black trousers, the ungainly sweater – it was as if she were purposefully trying to disguise herself, to defy the body that nature had given to her. Julie was running herself to seed, he thought, and he could not get away from the idea that she was doing it all just to spite him.
'Please go, Daniel. For God's sake, can't you respect even a simple request?'
'Not when you won't respect one of mine. What about Abel and Bob Davison? Why did you write to warn him?'
In his excitement he had climbed the lower part of the stairs himself.
'Daniel,' she said, retreating from him, 'get back. I'm telling you.'
'Not until I get an answer from you. What made you write that letter to Abel?'
'Because I happen to like him. He's the only part of your bloody family I've ever been able to understand. Now for God's sake get out of my house.'
She followed the command by running quickly up the few remaining stairs to her room. He stopped outside her door, momentarily aware that he had never let himself get carried away since she'd left him. He had always finally managed to persuade

himself into accepting Julie's independence, but this afternoon he was no longer able to do so. In order to justify himself he reflected that he hated what she was doing to herself, which in a way was exactly the same as saying that he hated what he had let her do to herself. If he had been stronger in the first place then none of this mess would have happened. He shouldn't have let her go. There was also the awkward nagging feeling that in spite of the afternoon's confrontation he wanted her, not just emotionally, but physically.

From inside the door he heard what he took to be the sounds of doors and drawers being opened and slammed shut again. The familiar banging and clatter was somehow reassuring, and after a time he demanded to be let in.

'Leave me alone,' she shouted back. 'You've no right to be here.'

'I have every right. I'm still married to you.'

She laughed aloud. 'You call this a marriage?'

'As far as the courts of England are concerned we are still man and wife.'

'I don't give a shit what the courts of England say.'

'Let me in, Julie. I have to talk to you.'

'No. No. No. No.' She banged on the door four times.

It was then that Daniel realised he was no longer alone. Standing behind him at the top of the stairs, the front door key still gripped in his right hand, stood a man he had known since his early childhood, a good friend of his father's. Charles Ponting. Ponting looked at him somewhat quizzically at first, then said, 'Daniel,' and held out his hand.

Charles Ponting had always played a shadowy role in his life. A lawyer by profession, he was a quiet man, slow in his speech and his movements. Even as a young child Daniel had thought of him as being bald, though he doubted that Ponting was now very much more than in his late fifties. Over the last year or two he had forgotten him, however, and this meeting threw him off balance.

It was pure habit that made him take his hand, embarrassment that made him drop it and say, 'I had no idea . . .'

'No, it's my fault. Julie obviously forgot to tell me that you would be here. Believe me, there's nothing I want less than to make things difficult.'

There was something humorous in that, and Daniel wondered if it wasn't intentional. Charles Ponting might be quiet and retiring in his private life, but he was quite different in the courtroom. There he was known for his unflinching, dogged determination. Rather short, slightly full at the waist, with what Daniel imagined to be rather fleshy hams and clean white legs, Charles Ponting reminded him of a well trained terrier.

What followed next was a very tense whisper from behind the door. 'If you two don't get out of this house immediately I'm going to open the window and scream blue bloody murder.'

Ponting looked across at him with his eyebrows slightly raised. With the hint of a smile he said, 'I think we'd better go downstairs.' Daniel followed without saying a word, noticing as they entered the living-room that Ponting seemed to know his way around. He walked across to the drinks cupboard and poured them each a Scotch. 'I think I ought to explain,' he said.

'You don't have to explain.'

'But I want to.' Daniel felt that he was being looked over and checked for weaknesses. 'Partly because we're old friends,' he continued in a more avuncular fashion. 'Partly because of the family link. And partly because it's not in my nature to leave things unsaid when in my opinion they need to be said.'

'You're having an affair with Julie,' Daniel blurted out.

There were twenty years between them. Daniel remembered Julie as a young girl, thirteen or fourteen perhaps, and Charles Ponting, both in the living-room at Rawley. A small, fair-faced man with light wisps of hair uneasily draped across his head. And Daniel's father. They were standing against the window, the young barrister and the elder Ross. Daniel remembered a china dog – pekinese – on the dresser. Charles wore a bow tie and he was speaking with quick but controlled gestures of the hands. Julie was in the corner on the floor, her hands filthy with coal. Daniel recalled the utter dismay on her face as she stared down at the black blotches over her hands and half way up her arms. Something, he forgot exactly what it was, had fallen in the coal scuttle, and without thinking she had reached in to get it. Seconds later she screamed with fury and leapt to her feet. The room fell silent and everything in it froze – and it was those frozen postures that Daniel remembered in such detail: his father, his head slightly bent, his fob watch loose from his pocket and dangling against his waistcoat; Charles, puzzled, his hands raised in mid-gesture; his mother, with her arms reaching out to the wretched girl, who in one final moment of despair had put her hands up to her face.

'No. I wouldn't want to call it an affair, Daniel. It wouldn't be right. The perspective would be all wrong.'

'You of all people,' Daniel said. 'Don't you realise that she's done nothing but play around ever since she left me?'

'You know that's not true. Julie had a difficult time after leaving you and she was very unsettled. Of course I understand that; one has to make allowances. But it was only for a while, and I think that you might try to appreciate the circumstances a little more fully. She didn't find it easy leaving you,' he added after a slight hesitation. 'You'd been married quite some time.'

'And we still are married . . .'

'Yes I know that. Legally, you are still married.'

Daniel spread his hands and watched Ponting as he stared into his drink. 'She won't be with you for long. This affair of yours. It won't last. I can promise you that.'

'I'm sorry, Daniel. I know it's a shock, and believe me I hadn't planned to sit down and talk about it today. In fact, I don't want to. But I think you should know that Julie and I go back a long way. Since before you were married.'

Daniel's mouth dropped as he looked for words. For a few seconds he felt he was being strangled by his own dumbness.

'No, not then,' Ponting said, as he realised what Daniel was thinking. 'It sounds like so much cant to talk about pure love, and I don't suppose anyone could love Julie in a pure way. But nothing happened between us while you were still together. I respected your privacy.'

For the first time Daniel felt Ponting's cold reasonableness choke on him. Aware of an unexpected urge to strike out at him, he realised that this was what he had really wanted to do ever since they had first known each other. There was something almost perfect about Charles Ponting which he had been educated to admire, but which some deep atavistic streak within him detested. Watching him, Daniel found himself wanting to despoil the scrupulously clean tabernacle in which Ponting lived.

'What do you want, Charles?' he asked at last. 'What do you expect?'

'Well, the two are very far apart. I can't say what I expect, but I know that I want to marry Julie. I want you to divorce her so that she can be free to marry me.'

Daniel laughed, but less out of amusement than of terror. 'You're twenty years older than her,' he said. 'And you don't understand Julie. She's got the appetite of a Paris whore and Catherine the Great rolled into one. You'd die of a heart attack within six months.'

Ponting grinned. 'You're making the same mistake about me as so many foreigners make about the English in general, Daniel, and frankly you should know better. Just because I appear to be a stuffed shirt doesn't mean that I am one.'

'And what does that mean?'

'For one thing, it means that three years have passed now and I'm delighted to be able to tell you that my heart is in first-class condition.' He watched as Daniel tried to grapple with this, then said, 'Please try to understand what's happened. I'm not trying to laugh at you.'

'It won't last,' Daniel muttered. Refusing to look across at him he added, 'It's me whom she'll come back to in the end.'

When he pulled himself together it was to see that Charles had gone. His drink, almost untouched, still stood on the small occasional table beside the chair in which he had been sitting. The door leading into the corridor was slightly ajar. From outside a church clock struck seven. Daniel stood up and went to the window. An evening in April. Even inside the room he could feel the chill in the air as a very light mist rose up from the river.

He was still standing there when Julie came down. A cigarette drooped from one hand. She had changed into a long but rather casual jersey dress and carried a handbag.

'Daniel,' she said purposefully. She sat down and stared at the carpet. 'I think we ought to have a talk.'

'What about?'

'About us.'

'You think I haven't tried to do that? Isn't that what I've been trying to do all these years?'

She looked up at him. 'I'm getting fed up of your coming round here and sitting on my doorstep.'

'Just tell me what I'm supposed to do. You don't answer my letters. You either put down the phone when you hear my voice or suddenly cut me off in mid-sentence. What else am I supposed to do? I've got to see you.'

'But you haven't. There's something, I don't know what it is, almost childish in you that won't face reality.'

'And what does that mean?'

'It means that we're not living together any more. It means that I don't particularly want to see you. We're bad for each other, Daniel. I'm bad for you and you're bad for me. Like what happened just now upstairs. It was awful. Like all those awful years of marriage.'

'You know that's unfair. All right, there were some bad times but then I'm not a bloody saint.'

'It was a farce,' she said wearily.

'You've no right to say that. You're just doing the usual, letting one or two isolated events twist your memory of the whole thing. Can't you get things into perspective for a change?'

'That's exactly what I have been doing. And I can see it all clearly for once. We don't need each other and we never did. It was just a habit, like so many other bloody awful marriages.'

He looked at her helplessly. 'That's totally untrue.'

'Why me, Daniel? There are plenty of other women who'd have you.'

The suggestion tormented him. For three years he had, with one exception, stayed away from other women, though whether out of fear or out of regard for Julie he would have been hard put to say. He told himself that it was because he felt there was something sacred about marriage, and it was this that made him say, 'You know I can't do that. I can't go around chasing other women, not while I still believe in our marriage.'

'The point is that I don't. I want out, Daniel.'

'And what does that mean?'

She shrugged her shoulders and half turned away. 'I want a divorce.'

'You want to marry Ponting?'

'Yes.' Her voice was barely audible.

'Jesus Christ.'

'You don't own me, Daniel.'

'He's talked you into it. Good God, Julie, you'll wake up one morning to find him stiff and cold in your bed.'

'There's no need to be obscene, Daniel. At least,' she said, 'it will make a change to being married to a perpetual adolescent.'

She stood up and he knew that the indication was that he should leave.

'Julie . . .' But whatever he had thought of saying remained unsaid. His mind was reeling. He was tired. The world was spinning too fast for him and he could hardly stand up. Julie's face clouded. He thought that he wanted to sweep her into his arms. He wanted . . . and it was only then that he realised that what he regretted most was not the loss of physical things, but the loss of affection. The thought stayed with him long after he had walked out into the chill of the evening air.

On Friday nights Daniel frequently went round to eat with Norma and Gordon Spence, but after leaving Julie he almost decided to forget dinner, go straight back to Rawley and then call Norma in the morning. After all it had been a long day and with the birth of Helga's baby in the morning he had the perfect excuse. But as he drove back out of London his thoughts drifted away from Julie and Helga. At some unknown but not too distant time in the future he would lose Rawley. After one hundred and seventy years the house would leave the family and become God only knew what awful complex – offices, a school, a convalescent home, perhaps. Rawley. He thought of its rooms, the vast attic he had known as a child, its stable yard and the great sweeping front lawn with the upturned marble vases and the crocuses lost at the bottom of the elm trees, and the grass and the trails of bramble that over the past few years he had allowed to break out untended from the old lines of ordered hedgeway. Memories of Rawley fought with the passing glare of oncoming traffic. The inside of the car filled with cigarette smoke.

As he turned into the lane that led home he stopped the car and got out. The moon was bright, about three-quarters full, and the wind, as he had expected from within that warm smoke-filled interior, was bitter cold. The truth was that it was not only Rawley he was losing but everything else as well. His wife. His brother. The Ross money of more than a century and a half had dwindled to almost nothing. Within ten years it would be gone, and he would more than likely find himself alone in a small brick bungalow. Standing there in that silence by the side of the car he knew that there ought to be a better ending to it all than this; the dreams and ambitions of five generations of Rosses deserved something more than this pathetic conclusion.

Perhaps, he was to tell himself later, it was the tiredness that made him take the road that led away from Rawley and turn off down the small farm track that led to the Spences'. Norma he had known since leaving Cambridge, a symbol of permanence in his life, and someone with whom he came into continuous contact through her work with charities. Gordon was a different matter. There was an antipathy between them, but one that had lost its cutting edge. Time had allowed them to fumble and grope for that plateau of understanding which allows habits and characteristics to be tolerated if not actively appreciated. In fact Daniel had never really liked Gordon, nor enjoyed the emptiness of feeling between them. He knew too that Gordon saw him as an anomalous left-over of another age, a museum piece. In his own words Gordon Spence was a product of the modern world, and he took a curious pride in his own existence. Yet in spite of the man's avowed socialist leanings Daniel had often felt that Gordon was but another example of the elitist masquerading under the image of the common man.

It was late when he arrived and they had obviously decided that he was not coming because Norma arrived at the front door with a napkin held up to her mouth.

'Daniel?'

She let him in and stood him up against the wall.

'You look awful,' she pronounced.

Norma had thickened with age, and though a couple of years older than him gave the appearance of someone already well into her forties. She dressed simply, and the hair gathered tightly on the back of her head would have made her face severe had there not been a permanent radiance about her that took one's attention away from anything else.

'You're here, anyway,' she continued. 'Whatever have you been doing to yourself?'

'Seeing Julie,' he said.

Norma stood back and said, 'I wondered if that wasn't it.' She rarely allowed herself to express her opinions about Julie, though he knew very well that she thought he was making a fool of himself.

'Norma. Wait.' He pulled her back from the doorway that led into the dining-room.

His grip on her arm was strong and as he swung her round she looked at him with pained surprise. 'Daniel? You're hurting me.'

He released her. 'I'm sorry.'

'What is it?'

'Julie. I want to know what she's said to you.'

'About you? Nothing. Now carry on in, they're waiting for you.'

'Has she said anything about us? About coming back to Rawley?'

Even as he said it he knew how ridiculous it was.

'What did she tell you, Daniel?'

'That she wants a divorce. But I don't believe her.'

Norma adjusted her hair slightly with one hand. 'I think you should.'

From her it sounded more acceptable. He lifted his head and asked, 'Have you two talked about it? About us?'

'Yes, we have.' She smiled and added, 'You're going to have to face facts someday, Daniel. You can't continue to let things go on like this for ever.'

He ignored the implications of the last comment and nodded towards the dining-room. 'Who's in there with Gordon?'

'Arthur.'

He was glad of that. He almost said, 'Thank God.'

Gordon and Arthur both looked up as he came in. They were sitting opposite each other. An empty place, his presumably, was set between them. He stood briefly in the doorway with Norma, now more noticeably tense than usual, standing beside him. It occurred to him that since Julie's departure he had spent much of his time in this house, especially in this room. It was a small room, set at one end of the house. Simple, like the house itself, and like their tastes. Gordon did not make much money as a lecturer at the local technical college, and Norma's had always been spent on the house and the few holidays they and the children managed to take away from England. Daniel knew how much these holidays meant to Norma. They were the one luxury in an otherwise monotonous existence. Yet she never complained.

'No more trouble from the workers these days, eh Daniel?' Gordon said with a grin as Daniel took his seat. Gordon was slight of build, with thin nervous fingers that were continuously active. They drummed at this moment lightly and persistently on the side of his wine glass.

'That's not very funny,' Daniel said, nodding at Arthur as he took his seat.

Arthur was perhaps the man whose friendship he valued most, and yet the person he was least capable of coming close to. His own relationship with Jenny, Arthur's wife, although devoid of any physical contact, nagged at him and he was plagued endlessly by the worry that one day Arthur would discover and come to the inevitable though wrong conclusion that they had been deceiving him. That Arthur had not found out Daniel put down to the fact that he was a secretive and retiring man, taken up completely by words – which he used as both armour and armament. Words were the means by which he safeguarded himself, surrounding him as they did with carefully labelled patterns. They were also the thread of Ariadne, the secret key by which the labyrinth could be conquered. Daniel had always felt a great affection for him, partly, he knew, because Arthur belonged very firmly to a civilisation that had been moulded largely by the impact of print, a civilisation to which he himself belonged and which he now feared was rapidly fading.

'Please, both of you,' Norma said, taking her own place at the table and carving briskly into the lamb. 'No politics. I forbid it.'

'Come on, Norma, it was a completely inoffensive question,' Gordon said, and there was just a slight hint of Yorkshire there which normally, and in complete contradiction to his beliefs on class and regional problems within the country, was well hidden beneath a very southern if rather clipped manner of speaking. 'I just wanted to know how things were getting on, that's all.'

'That's not what you meant, and you know it.'

Gordon laughed. 'Funny to think of the world without Ross's bread.'

'That's right,' Daniel said defensively.

'No more Ross's sticky buns.'

'Gordon!' Norma glared at him across the table.

'Well, you can't expect me not to take delight at the demise of yet another class oppressor, can you?' He grinned. Daniel knew that Gordon probably thought he was being humorous, though in all the years he had known him he had never really been able to establish just what he felt entitled to think of as funny.

'Frankly,' Daniel said, 'I'm relieved. It was a weight off my shoulders. I can use my energies better elsewhere.' Turning to Arthur he said, 'I see that Gordon's being his usual snotty self tonight.'

'He was worse before you came.'

Gordon snorted. 'Because I questioned Arthur's historical perspective. His last book was rubbish.'

'It wasn't rubbish,' Norma said, without looking up.

'Anyone who can make the statements and claims that he does should be locked up as potentially dangerous.'

'I made no claims,' Arthur said quietly. 'It was a novel. Nothing else.'

'A novel is never just a novel and nothing else.'

'You seem to forget that Arthur's an optimist,' Norma said. 'He doesn't believe in your simplifications about money and the world of capital.'

Daniel knew that it was very rare that Norma challenged her husband directly and he looked on the exchange with some amusement. However, he doubted that she would take it too far. The suspicion that he was being laughed at would soon prove too much and Gordon's mood would turn to anger. Daniel had seen him like that before; sullen, ugly, a man who knew he was out of control of what other people were doing and thinking and who was unable to tolerate the situation.

'Arthur is a sentimentalist,' Gordon continued, 'or rather a mentalist. One of these romantic individuals who believes in the divine and mystical powers of the will and other non-definable forces. The truth is that Arthur ignores what is happening politically in this country, the failure of management to make any meaningful contact with the labour-force, for example, and concentrates instead on people as though they exist apolitically, outside of the basic laws of capitalist enterprise. This being the case how do you expect me to take him seriously?'

'You aren't expected to, Gordon,' Norma said. 'But there are plenty of people who do.'

'Like Daniel,' he said with a smile.

'Yes, like me,' Daniel nodded.

'But then you're the product of the same way of thinking. And now your preoccupations define you. With the past. With that miserable and hypocritical apology for grandeur known as the British Empire. Or Rawley – that nabob's vineyard, built out of bribes and God knows what other evil when your forebears were pillaging India. And now, like my good wife, you attempt to erase the sins of the past by good works. Charity. My dear Daniel, you may well have good cause for a guilty conscience, but the way it works is unmistakably feudal.'

'That's enough,' Norma cut in sharply. Gordon subsided and went about his lamb truculently, fishing in the mint sauce with the end of his knife and playing like a child with his peas. Daniel looked at Norma's very steady and handsome figure set so squarely there at the end of the table and realised that Gordon, for all his beliefs, had not managed to even make a scratch on her. Even the children were like her – quiet, rather determined, and yet openly affectionate.

He was aware too of a sudden collapse of tension around the table, and in particular of a very strong warmth towards Arthur. He remembered their talking together two or three weeks earlier about the book he was working on and he knew instinctively that Arthur wanted to get out of the Spences' house and continue talking. Daniel could almost feel the heat rising up inside him; the Spences, their dinner table, their endless bickering, were things that Arthur wanted out of the way.

'Now tell me about the girl,' Norma said with sudden enthusiasm. 'What was her name? Helga, wasn't it?'

'She had a boy.'

'Marvellous. And they are both fine?'

Daniel thought of the child in the incubator. 'They're fine,' he said.

'And Abel?'

He felt then that Arthur was going to tell him something. He sensed him tauten, and for a while his presence was so strong it was as though he had actually gripped his arm. But seconds later the moment had passed and when he did speak it was only to ask for some more meat.

'I don't know.' Daniel looked across the table and realised just how lame the admission sounded to the others. 'He's disappeared.'

'You mean you have no idea where he is? And she doesn't know either?'

'She said she didn't care.'

'Silly fool. How does she think she's going to support the child? How old is she, seventeen or eighteen? Good God!' Norma lit a cigarette and stared at him. 'You never kept a tight enough rein on that boy, Daniel.'

'Perhaps you don't give her enough credit,' Gordon said. 'She can probably handle the child very well on her own. Besides, society's changing. The place is full of unmarried mothers.'

'I don't see that's a change for the better,' Daniel said.

'Better or worse, it's a logical situation which is bound to exist when people begin to reject marriage as the only proper place for having sex.'

The comment was followed by an uncharacteristic guffaw from Arthur, who said, 'They've been rejecting that proposition for centuries.'

'The men have, yes. But not the women.'

'Only if the men have sex by themselves,' Arthur hastened to point out.

'The point is that a young girl has given birth to a baby and she has no one to help her bring it up,' Norma interrupted. 'Of course, if Gordon had his way then it would go straight into a state crèche and be indoctrinated with whatever kind of rubbish the authorities cared to pour into it. Gordon's political opinions are mercifully irrelevant, but we are still left with a difficult situation which needs to be dealt with.'

'And just what, given the girl's nature, do you propose to do?' Gordon asked.

The point was well made. The conversation represented little more than dinner-table talk. The truth was that none of them was really in a position to do anything. Their feelings were irrelevant. Gordon smiled, then continued, 'I find the problem an interesting one, nevertheless. What would you suggest, Daniel? And what will you say to the malefactor, presuming, of course, that you can find him?'

'I don't hold him to blame,' Daniel said quietly.

'But I don't blame him. Abel, after all, is the product of his age. And what does the girl think of it all? Does she want to get married?'

'Not at all.'

'And doesn't that bother you?'

'That's my business,' Daniel answered tersely.

'But it does bother you, doesn't it? I would have thought that a situation like this would have put your precious ideas about marriage to the test.'

Norma reddened and pushed her chair back. 'Gordon, you're being objectionable. I wish you wouldn't drink so much.'

Daniel watched her pile up the dishes and remove them to the hatch that separated the dining-room from the kitchen. Marriage. As Norma walked across to the door he thought of Julie. And Arthur? What kind of marriage did he have with Jenny? But Arthur's face was neutral. He never spoke about his wife. Jenny, when pressed, would only laugh and say, 'Oh, Arthur and I are so different it would be impossible for us to live together all the time.' His thoughts drifted till he found himself thinking of Jenny Hallowes, alone in the small house that Arthur had bought for her in Putney, and the awkward, barren relationship that the pair of them had sneaked for so long behind Arthur's back.

'You know my views on marriage,' Daniel said finally, determined that Gordon should have an answer. 'I'm very upset by what has happened.'

That was all he said, though for a few seconds he found himself bewildered by a desire to strike out at Gordon, bewildered because this was for the second time in one day that it had happened, in spite of the fact that physical violence repelled him and he had long thought himself incapable of it.

When Norma returned she was bearing large cups of fruit cocktail which Daniel knew would have been laced with brandy. She appeared to want to ignore the confrontation that had taken place and blithely started to make plans for getting friends together to send things to Helga and the child.

Much to Daniel's surprise, however, as they were about to leave, and he had made arrangements to go back to Rawley with Arthur, Gordon took him aside and said, 'I think I ought to apologise, Ross.' He held him tightly by the arm and stared at him intently. Daniel was pinned against the clothes cupboard so that he was uncomfortably aware of an old fox fur of Norma's nestling its snout up against his neck. Gordon stood in front of him, swaying rhythmically, his thin hair scattered untidily across his head. 'I shouldn't have said all that.' He shook his head, looked at the floor and then concluded the encounter by saying, 'For God's sake don't go complaining to Norma. Don't mention it, eh?' He patted Daniel's arm, then careened off into the living-room where he fell into a chair with a copy of *The Times*.

Daniel remembered little of the drive home. It was late, sometime after eleven, and there was little traffic on the road leading to Rawley. As they pulled into the main drive and came to a stop outside the front door Arthur suddenly started chuckling, and it was only at this stage that Daniel was really aware that he was not alone. The moon was unusually bright and there was a strange luminescence from it which seemed to hang outside the windows of the car, as though suddenly frozen by the chill of the night air. Arthur sat without moving in his seat, his figure more like a wire sculpture than a solid mass of flesh and bone. But it was his face which really stood out. There was, in its quite alarming whiteness, the crevassed cheeks and the protruding ears that emerged like vast door handles through the thick, greying hair, something demonic, something of a medieval gargoyle.

Once outside the car they walked quickly across the gravel to the front door, and then stopped. Daniel put his hand out to steady himself against one of the pillars outside the door, struck by a feeling of unease that gripped him so quickly that it almost turned to panic. Abel. The intruder early that morning. The child, lying between life and death in the nursing home. And Rawley. He looked about him and felt the fear lift slowly. The house gave him something that at times he had privately called strength.

The house fell away to the left and right of them, with the night and the mist hiding its façade, its heavily decorated windows and the pillars that had been set into the full length of the front of the building. There was nothing like Rawley anywhere in the country, and yet there were pieces of Rawley which could be identified with every imaginative force that had existed in England over the last thousand years. Rawley was unique, and yet in its many parts was heir to a whole multitude of traditions. Daniel was proud of Rawley, proud of its strength, proud of his family's involvement with its existence. His life had started in one of its bedrooms. His childhood had been spent among its corridors and in the fields which it faced. His imagination had been formed by its endless variety. Rawley encouraged in him a sense of wonder – and yet at the same time a fear of the unknown. There was something in the detail of the place, in its very composition out of such varied tastes and materials, which at a very early age made him acutely aware of the nature of the physical world of which he was a part. More importantly, it created in him an almost awesome sense of the past and a fascination for the very varied forces and influences which converge out of the past to form one single moment in the present. Rawley had produced him, and yet it had also produced Abel. This was the contradiction which he could never resolve. Much as he told himself that he loved his brother, there was always a suppressed feeling that in creating a child who had nothing but contempt for everything the place stood for the house had somehow betrayed itself. However, with Arthur there with him he no longer thought of Abel; instead he was aware of some of the glow that he would at times feel when about to enter the house. The familiarity of the place warmed him and even outside he found himself anticipating what he already knew so well: the small cupola in the middle of the building, whose sole function was to shed light through its windows on the marble statue of Truth Overcoming Evil (Muse with outstretched hand and noble brow standing over the vanquished serpent), erected by his great-grandfather in the middle of the hallway; the endless suggestions of India and China, and other parodies of Regency eccentricity; the vast areas of gloom in rarely opened rooms where in quiet moments he had imagined children hiding, chamber-maids leaning against a wall to rest a little in privacy, and members of his own family reading letters six months old that had only just arrived from India.

As he pushed open the door he saw Polly standing by the telephone.

'Mr Daniel, thank God,' was all she said.

'Polly, what is it?'

She stepped back from the phone as though it had bitten her. For the first time in all the years he had known her she looked her age. However, she did not have to say very much. Her face told it all. Polly had just about brought up Abel single-handed since he had been two years old and she thought of him as her own child.

In the end it was Arthur who took the phone. When he finally put it down he stared at Daniel. 'He was brought in very ill. Barbiturates. A few days ago. They didn't know who . . .'

'Where is he?'

'They don't know. He discharged himself this morning. That was Bob Davison. He said he went across there as soon as he found out but Abel had already gone.' When Daniel continued to remain silent he added, 'I didn't know Davison was Abel's doctor.'

Daniel shook his head. 'He isn't.' He turned to Polly and saw that her face was broken, though she stood quite squarely and did not look away as his eyes met hers. For a time he was struck by the thought that there was something missing about her; it wasn't until much later that he realised that what he had been looking for was a duster in her hands.

When Daniel had known Bob Davison at Cambridge he had always been easy to like; self-confident, very relaxed, a person he was pleased to be seen with. There had always been an ornamental side to him. He put himself forward as decorative, extravagant in taste and manner, baroque. Good taste was not something that ever interested him. 'Good taste,' he would say, 'is a measure of those who seek to hide themselves, and frankly, Dan, that's the last thing I'm interested in. Mind you, there's nothing honest about good taste, believe me. The people who practise it are for the most part either frightened of what they see in others or frightened of what others see in them. As for myself, I don't care.'

The truth was that Bob Davison, whatever his outward affectations, cared very much about his chosen career. Cambridge for him was a place to make contacts, a place for self-embellishment, a place where a man could act the fool and yet be taken seriously. In fact, no one ever doubted that he would go far in the medical profession, and his later success caused little surprise. Daniel had sat somewhere on the outside of the coterie with which Davison had surrounded himself, prepared to do little more than quietly acknowledge his friend's gift for monologue and gratefully bask in the glow which arose from his energetic path through the university.

Few of Davison's original friends had witnessed the slow approach to middle age, the threatening obesity, the gradual dulling of the old fire, and the niggardly materialism which had accompanied his success, first as a surgeon and then as a consultant to one of the top London hospitals. Daniel was one of those who kept in contact, and though he too felt that somehow something more should have developed from such a magnificent beginning he refrained from the biting sarcasm that came from so many other quarters. Davison's homosexuality he preferred to ignore. There had never really been any proof. Besides, even if the allegations were true, he saw no reasons why a man should not follow his own nature as long as it caused no harm to others. Apart from that, he would reflect, the country had long since passed through the stage where it mounted witch-hunts. Confusion of a man's private and public sides, after all, ought not to be the product of a liberal society.

They met in Davison's Lancaster Gate apartment, and while his host busied himself on the telephone Daniel sat down and struggled to formulate what he wanted to say. No, he hadn't known that Abel had been taking drugs, but it was true that he had suspected it. Had he done anything about it? He thought about this for some time before answering himself by the thought that there was nothing that could be done. But as these questions and answers flashed past him, other more immediate queries struggled to the surface. Why Bob Davison? What was it that Julie had refused to tell him? Then perhaps he was worrying himself for nothing. Bob's presence was a coincidence. More than likely he had found out that Abel was in hospital through his colleagues and had gone there to visit him out of friendship to the family. It was a natural, human thing to have done. There was an answer. Why not accept it?

And Bob had changed. The old flamboyance had deteriorated. In the early days of their acquaintance things were fun, had been bought and possessed and handled because they were fun, because they irradiated some of the same irrepressible energy that had been such an essential part of Davison's youth. But not now. There was a precision to the room in which Daniel sat waiting, as Davison laughed and chatted noisily on the phone outside. The old richness had deserted the laughter; it was too high pitched and Daniel wondered uncomfortably if the performance out in the corridor were not somehow being staged for his benefit. Yet it was not so much the precision of the room and its contents that had shaken him so much as it was the sense of value, the sense of cost, the sense of physical things being exactly quoted, exactly placed, exactly labelled. Porcelain and china were carefully displayed within glass cabinets. Buddha heads from Angkor and Burma, statuettes from the Gupta period in India, figures that had been collected with care and were now neatly labelled, stating date and provenance and where purchased. The furniture was not the old, heavy and almost certainly valueless sets of chairs and tables which had made his early rooms so comfortable; there was a feeling of attenuation, of lines and angles displayed more for what they said for delicacy than what they represented of the human spirit. This same lack of the old bravado was evident in the miniatures hanging on the walls, the heavy silverware laid out prominently on a sideboard, but perhaps above all in the overall effect of a room robbed of breath by the multitude of small and fussy objects it had been forced to assimilate. There was a coldness in the place, a coldness reflected somewhat ironically, Daniel thought, in the small Japanese screen that had been placed in front of the old fireplace.

'Sorry, Daniel, but I'd made an appointment and with one thing and another I had to cancel the damn thing. You'll stay, won't you? Have lunch?'

Davison had thickened in the face and neck since Daniel had last met him, as though the body had made a crude attempt at some form of symmetry. He wore a striped shirt with a detachable collar, a long-time hallmark of his, the only real difference in his mode of dress being that whereas at one time the bow tie would have been outrageous it was now subdued.

'I should have come some other time,' Daniel said. 'But under the circumstances I didn't think you'd mind.'

'Of course not. I'm sorry, Dan. I really am. I know Abel's given you hell.'

Daniel's eyes flickered. He was tempted to refute the comment. Abel had worried him, it was true, but that didn't cancel out a brother's natural affection.

'What can you say?' Davison continued. 'What can any of us say? It's easy enough to make all the obvious comments, but that doesn't get us anywhere. Abel hurts because we know him, but I've seen it every day of my life for the past ten years. Perhaps I'm hardened, cynical.'

'I'm not looking for sympathy,' Daniel said. But what was it about Abel? He could never have him, never possess him. Was it simply that he couldn't bear to see his own flesh and blood denying everything that he had ever stood for? Or perhaps it was simply a matter of fear, he thought. Fear of the unknown. Fear of a future that had no barriers, the kind of future which lay in the hands of his brother and his brother's friends. But did they care? What did it all mean, all the machinery, the arrogance, the disregard for books, if at the same time they were indifferent to the alternatives of life and death?

'I want to understand why,' he said, looking across at Davison. 'I want to know.'

Davison chuckled. 'Still the same self-tortured liberal. You haven't changed a bit.'

'That's the way I am. The way I was brought up.'

'But don't fool yourself with sentimentality, Dan. You want Abel. You want him to be like you, because that way you can define him, close your eyes and pretend he doesn't exist. But you're not the only one.'

'Meaning what?'

'Perhaps we all want Abel to be like each one of us. Abel and all those others out there.' He lifted his hand and waved it lightly towards the window. He had sat down and crossed his legs, legs that had always been short and thick so that now one thigh sat uneasily on top of the other while the trousers rode up from the ankle to reveal several inches of white and hairless calf. 'Arthur, for example.'

Davison said those last few words quietly, then bent to examine his nails. After a while he looked up and smiled as he met Daniel's blank but troubled face.

'Arthur's afraid of Abel. So afraid that it's almost a mania. But you probably know all this,' he said. When Daniel continued to remain silent he said, 'It comes, of course, from Arthur's total reliance on words and his rather emotional attitude towards language. Abel and his band of troopers he sees as the vanguard of a new wave of Goths. Arthur fears the end of civilisation; he fears the burning of Rome. Bloody nonsense of course, but then Arthur's philosophy was always a shambles. Christ knows how anyone lets him get away with it.'

'You never did like him,' Daniel said defensively. 'And in many ways you know that I respect his beliefs.'

Davison nodded then pushed his hands across his cheeks. 'I had a bad night, Dan, wondering just what I should tell you. Wondering how you would react.' He looked up, as though he were appealing for Daniel's assistance. 'You know yourself that Abel's not a particularly stable person. I'm not saying that you didn't do the best for him. You did. But his background, the lack of mother and father . . .' he broke off, and in a lighter tone said, 'I want you to know that I don't hold you to blame.'

'For what?'

'For what happened. The truth is that Abel could do without that maniac friend of yours writing to him, which he does, constantly. Confronting him, which he has done several times. It's the attempt to mould, that's what I'm getting at. You all wanted to mould Abel, so much so that he's almost no idea who he is.'

Daniel felt threatened by the entire performance. He resented Bob Davison's manner; he resented the criticism; he resented the dislike the man had always had for Arthur Hallowes, a dislike which he knew stemmed from a time a few years earlier when Arthur had incorporated a delightful send-up of the younger Davison in one of his books.

'I take it you've seen quite a bit of Abel, then,' Daniel said. He found to his consternation that his voice was shaking. Tiredness, he told himself. He was still tired and overwrought. Davison had done what any decent man might have done. If Abel had wanted to confide in someone, as Davison seemed to be suggesting had been the case, then what better than that he should confide in an old family friend?

'Yes. He'd come. Talk. Things that perhaps you and he could never really get down to, Dan. The way your own role was so ambiguous. I think Abel always tended to see more of the father-figure in you than anything else; and in some ways I think that's what he wanted to see. Unfair on you, of course. I know that.'

Daniel nodded. It made sense, even if in some ways it was too neat, too easy an explanation. But it was true that Abel resented his intrusion, while at the same time appearing to spend so much of his time actively seeking it.

'What were they?' Daniel asked. 'The things that worried him?'

Davison coloured, and then in a subdued voice said, 'Jenny. He'd talk about her a lot. You and her.'

Daniel kept silent, waiting to see how Davison would continue.

'He couldn't understand how . . .'

'I didn't know he knew.'

'For God's sake, Daniel. The boy's got eyes. Everybody knows.'

Daniel stood up and walked to the window. 'This is ridiculous, Bob. There's nothing to know. Nothing. Nothing at all.' He looked around swiftly.

'But he knows you see her.'

'And what does that prove? I see the grocer and the milkman, for that matter, but it doesn't mean that we're playing games together.'

Davison sniggered and the interjection caught Daniel off-guard, was so out of place that the only word he could think of later to describe it was obscene.

'All right,' Davison allowed, 'so there isn't anything. But that's not the way it looks, and it's not how Abel sees it.'

'What did he say?'

Davison shrugged his shoulders and Daniel felt him trying to back down. 'Does it really matter?'

'Yes. To me it does.'

'He didn't say much. Now, he hardly mentions it.' He looked up helplessly, but Daniel was struck later that there was the faint suggestion that he was actually enjoying himself. 'He said he couldn't understand how you could go on about Julie while you were screwing someone else's wife on the side.'

Daniel shook his head in violent denial. 'He's wrong. It's never been like that. I've never wanted it to be like that.'

But he had, and Abel had known, had watched him over the

meal table and seen how he'd struggled with images of Jenny Hallowes, fighting them off at first, but always in the end giving in. Jenny at night. Jenny beside him in the car. Jenny. Images of her poured out of his imagination endlessly, taunting him with sudden and reckless desire in the most public places, mocking, and vibrant with immediacy.

'Not with Arthur around,' he continued. 'I know you don't appreciate his books, Bob,' he said with an attempt at laughter, 'but I do. And I respect him as a man. Even if Jenny and he don't spend all the time together I have to respect their marriage.'

'Why?'

Daniel was staggered to see that Davison was openly amused.

Not respect, Daniel, he heard himself say. Fear. Fear of the consequences. Fear of a pattern broken. Fear, like Arthur's fear, of being stranded suddenly with the thread severed and the journey home no longer a possibility.

The unease continued with him for the rest of the day and followed him back to Rawley in the evening. Once there, however, the familiarity of things long known and the inescapable suggestiveness that was part of their quality calmed him down. The place was unusually quiet, the lights not turned on. Polly's day off, he remembered. Without her the place was like a mausoleum. Once in the hallway he hesitated as he was about to climb the stairs. For a brief moment he saw movement at the top. He stopped. His mother. Lowering his head into his hands he pressed his fingers hard into his eyes. Tiredness. He was distraught. Perhaps he should have asked Davison for medical advice. The thought made him smile and he was still smiling when he looked up again and found himself staring at the projected figure of his mother as she'd stood that day at the top of the stairs.

It had been the morning of Coronation Day, nineteen fifty-three. When his mother had appeared that morning on the stairs she was wearing blue. Her dress was long; it fell in gently caressing folds about her figure, sweeping easily off her hips in cascades of shining cloth till it just brushed the floor. She held one hand on the banisters as she came down the stairs, but not gripping it as a man might grip a support, not with the fist clenched and the fingers taut, but with the palm slightly arched and the fingers doing little more than touching the wood, as though they were engaged in an extraordinary interchange of energy with it. As she moved the dress rippled. He remembered being struck by the way her movement seemed suddenly to blend itself into a far greater sense of rhythm that involved the entire hallway – the great square flagstones, the solid walls with their pictures of generations of Rosses long dead and buried, and the dome of the cupola above, stained as it was by birds, but nevertheless still throwing down beams of light on to the statue of Truth Overcoming Evil.

Daniel had been standing to one side of the statue and was surprised to see her smiling as it was unlikely that she could have seen him. Yet as she left the stairs her smile broke into a gushing laugh that amazingly filled the entire hallway with its gaiety. He shrank back, wondering what he had done to cause this unprecedented change in his mother, only to realise that it wasn't him at all whom she was looking at but George Hutchinson, and to whom she now ran with her arms open.

'George,' she sang out. 'How marvellous to see you.'

She stopped just a foot or so short of him, and wilted. The whole sequence had been so surprising that it had left Daniel at a loss as to what might happen next. It was as though at one moment his invalid mother had been taken over by some supernatural life force only to have the same gift just as suddenly withdrawn.

George Hutchinson held a special place in these memories of those early years at Rawley. He had arrived that morning wearing a blue corduroy suit that bulged and hung around and about his enormous girth, so that when he was walking he seemed from the back like a vast and colourful bolt of cloth. Corduroy was George's material, as sombre black and grey flannel was his father's. He wore it with abandon, transformed into jackets, trousers, waistcoats and even slippers. He owned wardrobes full of suits; suits of blue and black, orange and burgundy corduroy. Why he liked the material so much Daniel never discovered, but its richness suited him; it complemented his expansive nature, and when it refused to retain its creases, when it sagged and spread, it seemed to point to a certain ease which was always about him, and the dislike he had of cant and pomposity.

George was always conscious of himself as an Englishman. His mind was an encyclopedia of things English, of English men and women, of their poems and their music, their paintings and their speech, their strange intuitions and their achievements in the more practical world of machines and business. This knowledge and obsession (because George was totally obsessed by England, as much as another fellow-countryman might find himself obsessed by steam engines, or gardens, or beer) stopped at the boundaries of the country. It did not cross into Wales or Scotland. It knew nothing of Ireland. George was a true Anglo-Saxon, whose passions in the end would do little more than take up his own time. In fact, he was never particularly interested in convincing others of his opinions, however much he liked to express them. The very act of expression was not for the sake of contention, but for the very simple sake of living. George Hutchinson, and for that matter his father as well, quite simply lived a life which was totally self-absorbed and yet without pretension.

It had been a surprise to see his mother approach George so openly and with such flaunted affection, for this was neither his way nor hers. Women were a peripheral factor in his existence; it was the company of men that he sought, and in particular Daniel's father. Both of them lived largely in the past, and for Daniel their preoccupations with the past had sunk deep into every crack and corner of the house. The rooms and corridors were haunted by their conversations, which in fact were really confrontations that had almost nothing at all to do with the exchange of ideas. Rather, they were great passages of time – three or four hours at least, accompanied by glasses of Scotch or brandy – filled with all kinds of facts and figures. Dates of executions. Dates of invasions. Dates of births. Accessions and deaths of monarchs. The decease of princes, aunts, uncles, pet dogs and cats. Records of weather, including hailstorms, rainstorms, thunder-claps, electrical discharges, ruination of crops, the incidence of fog, smog, the wrecks on the Goodwin Sands and the breaking up of the sea walls on the south coast. Opinions of men and women, their capacity to lead, to follow, to drink, to eat, and their courage in living and dying (especially, Daniel recalled the deaths of Raleigh, Charles the First, Mary Queen of Scots, Lady

Jane Grey, More, Laud, and the bishops Latimer and Ridley). Opinions and incidents relating to courage and conquest, with especial reference to India, but also not forgetting the great individuals who followed their own leads and defied either Whitehall, the East India Company, or accepted convention. As early as the age of seven or eight Daniel became familiar with the names of Burton, Clive, Frobisher, Gilbert, Scott, Napier, Nelson and Drake. Nor were the names of the great poets and writers omitted from these sessions. Their names were flipped across the room, their deeds recorded, their poems quoted, their rollcall read out like pages of fact from *Bradshaw* or *Michelin's Guide*. There was never an end to the exchange of anecdotes, of English men and women called out from the depths of time and made to dance and cavort for the sake of these two totally obsessed individuals in the middle of the twentieth century. They would sit, Ross in his heavy black boots, the fob watch more than likely loose from his pocket and his moustache just wet from his drink, and Hutchinson bundled up in his corduroy, his limbs moving endlessly beneath his chair, and continue these exchanges for hours without being aware of time or even of their audience. Daniel was for years nonplussed by these antics and it was only very much later that he realised that, in contrast to all appearances, his father and George Hutchinson had in fact been communicating at a very deep level of the spirit – that a conversation which might involve an account by one of W. G. Grace at the wicket followed by a summary from the other of *David Copperfield* amounted to a tacit understanding that the world was far too complicated a place to talk one's way out of, and that all that was possible was the indulgence of one's likes and dislikes in the company of someone who would not interrupt.

Bringing himself back to the present, Daniel turned and reached for the hallway lights. He grunted as he dismissed the memories that so preoccupied him. His mother, his father, George Hutchinson. They were all dead.

He was about to continue up the stairs when he stopped, certain that he was not alone in the house.

'Polly?' he called out. 'Are you back so soon?'

Looking around him he saw that the library door was open. As he stepped through it he felt that he knew in advance what had happened. Even so, the absolute havoc in the room, the hundreds of books mauled and torn on the carpet, swept across his desk and flung against the chairbacks as though driven under the impetus of some unrestrained force, stopped him in his tracks. The awful power that had destroyed what to him was the very centre of the house seemed to throw itself at him, so that for a few seconds he was left without the slightest ability to respond. When it lifted he was so weak that he could hardly raise his feet. He moved awkwardly into the centre of the mess, his feet soiling already torn and useless pieces of paper. *Daniel Deronda. Bleak House. Little Dorrit.* Sterne. Disraeli. Trollope. Bentham. Mill. Many of the books he remembered individually: knew where he'd bought them, who'd given them to him. One of my saner investments, he'd tell his guests. And it had been a collection to be proud of. He was never ashamed of his pride in his books; it had always seemed so harmless.

The destruction was almost complete. Hardly a single book remained on the shelves; even the shelves themselves were splintered in places, as though they had been hacked with an axe. When he reached his desk he sat down and stared at the window. The police? What could they do? But it was a criminal act, a senseless act of destruction against private property. The individual was protected against that. He's harmless, Helga had said. Harmless. Daniel laughed, and for several seconds the strained tones of his laughter bit savagely into the otherwise still confines of the house. When he had finished he stood up and looked about him.

'Edgar!' He shouted out the name, then listened to it die away.

The certainty that he was being watched unnerved him. He turned slowly on his heels.

'I'm willing to talk,' he said. The words danced around the room. About what? Abel? Jenny? His wife? The shadows of his father and George Hutchinson playing games with the names and exploits of other people?

The silence persuaded him of what he had felt for a long time. There was no longer any time for talk. And perhaps no point. But he'd done nothing to deserve this. Had he? The question repeated itself endlessly, a whirlpool that obeyed no laws outside of its own self absorption.

Night fell. When Polly returned she found him asleep, his head lying on the desk, a half empty bottle of whisky beside him.

Julie had only been down to Rawley four or five times since leaving Daniel, and on each occasion her arrival had been preceded by elaborate arrangements over the phone and by letter. This time she arrived unannounced. The first Daniel knew of it was when she braked hard on the gravel outside the front door, and the conversation held in subdued tones with Polly in the hallway. Polly had never particularly liked Julie, but Daniel wondered if her urge to gossip might not overcome her feelings and lead her to tell Julie about what had happened to the library. He'd had some trouble overcoming Polly's initial reactions, but in the end had persuaded her that he didn't want the police or any publicity whatsoever. What he couldn't tell her was that the incident had made him feel shame rather than anger: shame at his own impotence, at his complete inability to cross the gap that separated himself and those who had vandalised his home. The destruction of his books was an act of violence against himself; it had left him disgraced.

'It's Mrs Ross, Mr Daniel,' Polly said, pushing open the door to the living-room and showing Julie in.

Julie stood a little uncomfortably in Polly's shadow, then walked quickly into the room. She looked tired and in some ways more homely than he had ever seen her before. It had always seemed impossible that one day Julie might start to show signs of age, but they were there now. The eyes were tired and heavy. There was a lack of vitality in the way she walked.

Polly continued to stand smugly in the doorway before

announcing her departure by saying, 'You look very well, Mrs Ross. Much better.'

Julie ignored the comment, sat down and said, 'Surprised?'

'A little. Perhaps too numbed to register much surprise.' He wondered what had brought her.

'I want to apologise,' she said. 'The other day. I've not been very sympathetic.'

She lifted her face so that the light across it shifted the image suddenly to a summer afternoon when, out walking by himself, he'd come across Walter Perkins's daughter, naked, sunning herself, with a book lying open across her stomach. Later on that evening he'd asked his mother about her. There was a reluctance in the family to talk openly about Perkins, or even mention his name. They had sold the land to him because they needed the money, then watched with unease and disapproval as he had put the first of his houses on pasture and woodland that had once been part of the old estate. His mother had looked at him knowingly and said, 'Julie. At least that's what I think he calls her.'

'No, it's not you,' he said. 'I can't stand in your way any more, Julie. I've acted badly.'

She watched him carefully, sensing that something had either happened or was in the process of happening that he was keeping from her.

'I suppose it's natural to cling,' he said, then stopped as if uncertain how to go on.

He poured them each a drink and sat down, hoping that she wouldn't force him to talk.

'I heard about Abel,' she said. 'Have you been able to find him?'

He shook his head. 'I went to see Bob Davison. Nothing. He doesn't know where he is, either.' A little later he asked, 'Why did you warn Abel about him, Julie?'

'Simple. I don't like Bob Davison. I never have.'

'But that shouldn't make any difference. He's a human being like you and me. What he does privately isn't our affair.'

'Oh Christ, Daniel, you're so bloody insipid when it comes to reacting to the real world. I'm not talking about what you ought and ought not to do or feel. I'm a practical person who likes getting involved with real things. I don't give a damn about hypothetical moral issues, only about what I know and see.' She laughed. 'How you and I ever thought we'd make it together I don't know. I sometimes wonder if human chemistry wouldn't do better with a little programming.'

Daniel heard her out, then surprised himself at just how easily he found himself accepting the inevitability of the divorce. She was right. They should never have married. It had been a mistake. He felt the words tick off in his mind like a meter slowly turning over.

'I still think that Bob's a decent person,' he said. 'I didn't know that Abel had spent so much time with him, but I'm glad, now that I do know.'

Julie eyed him seriously. 'You're an idiot, Daniel Ross. Bob Davison is a shark. A collector. He'll gobble up your brother and then spew him out clothed in silk panties and wearing lipstick.'

He flushed and turned away to hide his embarrassment. Julie's language had always been theatrical, something that he'd found amusing at first but which was so often turned against him that he'd learnt to fear it.

'You're forgetting Abel,' he said, determined to face her. 'Remember the letters? The magazines?' He laughed, praying that she'd laugh with him, that now she was with him something of the old life would come back.

She nodded. 'Yes, perhaps I am. I'm sorry, I didn't mean to be so crude.' Then after a slight hesitation she said, 'I spent the night thinking. About us. About you and Rawley, and your funny preoccupations. Sometimes I find myself wondering . . . but I don't like sentimentality, and that's what it is. There's no way for us to start again, Dan. But that doesn't mean I'm going to try to forget the past. There's far too much of us to do that.'

She stopped and he was surprised to see her uneasiness, to see her struggling for words.

'You're going to marry Ponting?' he asked.

'Yes.'

'Lucky old Charles.'

'Please don't be bitter about it.'

'Oh, you know me, Julie. Good old free-thinking Daniel Ross. You know I'm only too pleased to let Charles have a go.'

He lit a cigarette, his hands shaking. Then, as he looked up, it was to remember the books lying across the floor, and the fear he had tried to drown in the whisky, the fear he'd had all his life of physical and emotional pain.

'I suppose you haven't seen my father?' she asked. That was it. He told himself that this was the real reason she'd come down to Rawley. It made more sense than her original explanation; Julie would never have come down simply to apologise for her behaviour.

'He doesn't know about Ponting?' Daniel asked.

She shook her head. Daniel remembered his early contact with Walter Perkins. Small, ferret-like, scrambling – there had always seemed something vaguely unpleasant about him. But there was an energy in him, a restless rooting energy that had driven him to success, which in his case meant the blossoming of his building company and the mushrooming of low-quality housing estates over the southern counties. In fact, Daniel had been surprised by Perkins, not just at how shrewd he was but at his warmth and his apparent disregard for convention. Over the years a wary friendship had grown up between the two men, one that Julie had respected and even, Daniel suspected, had attempted to foster. As an only child she had come to find her father's attentions, his constant presence, his worrying that she was getting the best and only the best, too claustrophobic, and Daniel had wondered at a very early stage if she had not thought that her father might not transfer some of this attention to him. It was certainly true that a bond had developed very quickly, for Walter Perkins had shown a deep respect for what he called 'scholarship' but which could also have been translated as the ability to talk about books, films and relationships between events and people which were of no immediate concern to the business of every-day living.

From the very start Perkins had nosed his way inside Daniel's head and started rooting about for information and opinion. He was like that. A man who had poured every ounce of himself into his business and his daughter. And yet, as Daniel looked at Julie, with her father's jutting chin and his thrust of the shoulders, he knew that she had shied away from him. There was a coldness about her which he did not have, and though his emotions were rarely on display it was obvious to Daniel that there was an element of loneliness in the man which his daughter was either unaware of or merely ignored.

'It'll be a shock,' she said. 'Dad always did like you. Part of a deeply ingrained working-class respect for the local squire, I expect.'

'Respect?' Daniel laughed. 'I always thought he took great pleasure in Parklands. As though he wanted to wipe Rawley off the map.' Daniel thought of the new section of the village with its central school and its planned facilities, all of which Walter Perkins had marked indelibly with his stamp.

'No. He likes you. And I haven't been very good to him, I know that. But the reason he won't like the divorce is because of what happened before.' Although Julie had never spoken openly about what had happened with her mother he knew the strength of feeling she was referring to in her father. 'Perhaps it's his old age, I don't know, but he's become something of a fierce moralist when it comes to what he feels should and should not happen between men and women. So, he'll see you as wronged. The old pattern reasserting itself. And though he'll smile and talk to me, he'll never forgive me.' She tossed her head, then in a strained voice said, 'It's funny how some people can get away with it, isn't it? How do you do it, Daniel?'

The brittleness in her voice cut into him. 'What do you mean?'

'You think I don't know what's been going on?'

Jenny. It had to be. 'No, you don't understand,' he said in quick denial. 'You've got it all wrong.'

'How is she? I suppose there must be a certain frisson doing it with the wife of one's friend. Not that I don't admire you, darling. I think your twofacedness one of the most miraculous and extraordinary revelations to have come out of all these long years. Really. You had me fooled. Completely.'

She smiled, but there were tears in her eyes. He watched helplessly as they streamed down her face.

'Julie,' he said, and went forward to her. The anger, her shame, she'd kept hidden completely ever since walking through the door, and perhaps, he thought, she had even intended not bringing the subject up.

'No, Daniel. There you were, nodding and cackling away about my guilt for three years, fawning over me, begging me to come back, implying God only knows what magnificent forgiveness for the prodigal on her return, when all the bloody time you've been humping that skinny bitch. For Christ's sake, where did you learn such extravagant hypocrisy?'

Daniel watched her back towards the door. 'There isn't the slightest physical relationship between Jenny Hallowes and myself,' he said. 'Nothing. I haven't touched her, not even once.'

She shook her head in disbelief. 'It doesn't matter. Not now.'

'What doesn't matter?'

She dried her eyes carefully, then reached inside her handbag for her cigarettes. 'I'm sorry, Dan. I didn't mean to bring it up. I don't know what made me say it. I left home this morning telling myself that I wasn't going to mention it. But it hasn't been easy. Watching this place fall apart. Wondering if you'd ever come to your senses. If you'd ever open your eyes long enough so that you might actually catch a glimpse of what's really going on in the world outside. Wondering if there was ever a chance, and knowing, knowing but not wanting to know, that there wasn't a dog's chance in hell.'

He heard her only vaguely. She still hadn't answered his question and he repeated it. 'Julie, what is it that doesn't matter?'

She looked up, then shrugged her shoulders.

'I told him,' she said.

'Told who?'

'Arthur.' She spoke the name quietly, then as if to add emphasis she said, 'I told Arthur about you and Jenny. You made me so bloody angry, Daniel. I'm sorry.'

They would talk to Arthur, both of them confront him and have the whole thing out in the open. That was the decision he'd come to after hours of deliberation once Julie had left him to return to London. Why Julie had told Arthur he couldn't understand, but then the display of emotion had been unlike her also. Jealousy? It was impossible to think that she was capable of it. Or perhaps it was nothing more than a simple desire to hurt him. His mind refused to dwell on the situation for very long; he felt abused and cheapened by what she'd done and he found it easier to push it as far out of his thoughts as possible. The presence of a real problem helped, however. No matter what had caused Julie to act that way, he still had to get things straightened out with Arthur. After all, Julie was wrong; there was no affair. His relationship with Jenny, sad and strained though it might be, had never been conducted inside the bedroom. That was fact. Jenny was a friend, a confidante, someone he felt he could talk to. They read books together, would go to plays, then return to her place and talk about them endlessly over cups of coffee. And he liked to think that he gave her something she needed. He saw her as a retiring sort of person, shy and wary of other people, and without Arthur around with no one to share her curiosity and interests. It was, however, a fair exchange, because he was flattered that someone of her intellect and ability should find so much pleasure in his company. He felt himself relax when he was with her, yet at the same time she boosted his ego and made him feel that his concerns were important. Although he'd always been worried how Arthur would take their friendship, he'd never wanted to include him as a way of legitimising the relationship; it was impossible for him to get away from the desire to have Jenny to himself, even in the non-physical and frustrating manner which he had settled for.

As he turned off Putney High Street and slowed down to a stop outside the house that Arthur had bought for her, she came out of the front door, very much as though she had been waiting for him.

'You see, I expected you,' she said. Daniel smiled instinctively. There always seemed something right about his coming home to Jenny. It was not that he had ever felt he'd wanted to marry her or even live with her. She'd never had that power over him. There was a frailness about her; her lips were pale, her fingers delicate and her figure lithe, almost boylike. There had always seemed to him something incongruous about her with Arthur, because where she was elflike, Arthur, with his tall plodding body, gave the impression of clumsiness. One expected him to fall into things, to be unable to establish any kind of working rhythm with those objects that crowded his environment. But there was a simple flow to Jenny's movements. She lived with ease among her possessions. She even lived with ease among these streets, these unbending brick and bow-windowed terraces, with their uncompromising arrogance and their suggestions of Non-conformist meanness. What was so right was that he felt he could respond with sympathy to her frailty, her simple liberalism, her very ordinariness. What he liked in her was what he felt he ought to display in himself.

'You haven't called for ages,' she said, as they went in.

He told her about Helga and she listened patiently before saying, 'You know that she left the hospital?'

He did not try to hide his surprise. 'When?'

'Last night. I went down there, oh, just to take some things.' She smiled easily.

'That was very thoughtful of you. You shouldn't have . . .'

'You know me, Dan. I was at a loose end and besides I thought that she might like the company.'

'Did they say where she'd gone?' Then remembering the

child, he added, 'But the kid was still in the incubator, wasn't it?'

She nodded. He noticed a distance in her look which was unusual in her, as though her mind were totally occupied elsewhere.

'She abandoned the child?'

'I suppose you could call it that.' There was an uneasy silence following that, which she ended by adding, 'But Helga never wanted the child anyway, did she? I mean isn't that what you said?'

'Not in so many words.' He thought of the child. His own name. 'What a bloody mess,' he said suddenly.

He remembered talking to Jenny about the situation before Helga had gone into hospital. She'd been interested, he'd recalled. Had asked about her relationship with Abel. In fact she'd shown so much interest that he'd teased her about wasting her life. What she really ought to be doing, he'd told her, was social work.

'So I suppose she's gone back to Abel,' Jenny said next.

'Abel? God, I don't know. I don't even know where the bloody boy is.'

He sank back in the chair and wondered how he was going to tell her what Julie had done.

'Poor old Daniel, you deserve better.' Jenny's homilies and set pieces came as easily and just as unaffectedly as a comment on a film, or a criticism of government policy. He liked that about her, the way she'd dispense opinion so casually and with such apparent disregard for degree or importance. 'Shall I make some coffee?' she asked. 'You look worn out.'

'Yes, coffee. And yes, I'm tired.'

'Just today?'

'No. It all seems to be happening at once.'

'You have a great capacity for understatement, Dan.'

'Yes, perhaps it's my only gift,' he said jokingly.

She laughed as she went out to the kitchen. He felt more at ease than he had done initially, though it had always been difficult to relax completely when he knew that he was really in Arthur's domain. The house had been bought with his money. His money had bought the simple furniture, had paid for the walls to be redecorated and the prints and paintings which Jenny had hung on them, and his money too that had paid for the television and the deep freeze. None of this could he forget, any more than he could forget that Jenny was still Arthur's wife. Jenny had never really said what she felt about Arthur – words such as love, marriage, even faith and honour, didn't exist in her vocabulary, and there were times when he felt that she went deliberately out of her way to avoid them. Not that Arthur's own preoccupation with her wasn't there in his books for everyone to see. Jenny was all women to Arthur. A mother figure, a lover, a child. Yet Daniel knew that the real flesh and blood woman was in many ways far too great a reality, and it was this reason which he accepted for the time that Jenny would spend away from her husband in Putney. The truth was that Jenny frightened him, and so he had rehewn her, cut her this way and that, shaping her to his own liking almost a dozen times over. The fictionalised Jenny was in many ways his best creation.

It was only when she returned with the coffee that he noticed that her movements were awkward, as though certain parts of her body were stiff or in pain. Genuinely puzzled by this he was about to ask her if she felt all right when he realised that she had noticed his attention and seemed embarrassed.

'Jenny? What is it?'

Her faced flushed a deep red. She turned and faced him, her eyes wide and staring. And then he noticed what seemed to be part of a weal, running just across the collar-bone before it dipped and vanished beneath her blouse.

'It's nothing. Really. Nothing at all.' Her voice was so quiet that he could hardly hear what she'd said.

He stood up, went across to her and raised his hand gently to her shoulder. She flinched, then moved back, shaking her head. There was a puffiness too about her eyes, although she'd obviously spent some time working on them before he'd arrived.

'What happened?' he asked her.

'He came,' she said simply. Her hands hung limply by her sides. It was more of a whisper than anything else. He felt her waiting patiently.

'Who?' he asked.

'Arthur. Who else?'

'And he did that?' He was distracted momentarily by a small brooch pinned to her breast. Silver. A swallow.

She nodded. 'He was drunk. Does that surprise you?'

It was impossible, that was the first thing that crossed his mind. Arthur was incapable of hurting her; he hated violence. His whole work was an odyssey against violence, a monumental effort by one man to put forward and honour what was best in human nature. He despised television and cinema for capitalising on greed, sex and acts of violence. Arthur did not see mankind that way, and he deplored the cynical majority that did.

'Because of us,' she said. 'You and me.' She continued to keep her eyes on him, and in the end it was he who looked away.

'I don't believe it.'

She turned sharply and in a tone that he was quite unused to in her said, 'It's your privilege not to have to believe.'

He kept his eyes on her, incapable of movement. It was almost as though she were making him watch her. Slowly and hesitantly at first, but the more deliberately, she pulled the blouse out of the top of her skirt. As she continued to pull the buttons separated, and he turned away.

'And you don't want to believe, do you?' she taunted him. He turned back to her. There were bruises on her ribs and a long red tear across her left breast. She stood quite still, her top half completely naked, her head slightly lowered. Her hair fell forwards so that he could see the red and black marks of his fingers imprinted on the back of her neck and round the back of her shoulders. As if in response to some hidden signal she raised her head again and looked at him. Her face was expressionless. The pale blue eyes, now held quite still, the lightly coloured lips, the fine angle of her lower face, all seemed dead.

He wanted to say that it wasn't Arthur's fault, but then it was obviously ridiculous to blame Julie. Excuses followed on, though, each one of them begging to be accepted, each one turned away as facile and irrelevant. Arthur had been drunk. Overtired. Disgraced to the point of frenzy by what he might have interpreted as treachery.

'I'm shocked,' he said.

A slight smile appeared for a brief moment. Her eyes lit up. She turned away. Daniel saw none of it; he stared at her naked back, and deprived of the power of speech, moved towards her. He lowered his mouth to the back of her neck and kissed her, at first hardly knowing what he was doing, then as he lifted his hands to her back and pushed them round to her breasts, more urgently.

She closed her eyes and her body tightened. He noticed nothing at all until he swung her round and reached for her lips with his mouth. It was only then that he looked at her and saw the stress marks round the mouth, the rigid retreating body, and the look of panic in her eyes.

It was when he withdrew from her that he fully appreciated what had happened. For the first time in all the years they'd known each other he'd allowed his desire for her to break through, and it had needed this, he realised with horror, the marks on the flesh and the crushing revelation of what Arthur was capable of and perhaps even had done on earlier occasions, to bring it about. However, he was still too concerned with his own reactions to understand what feelings might lie behind her rejection of him. He stepped back to the door and only turned when she called his name.

'Don't be hurt,' she said, and there was a sudden lift of spirit in the voice that arrested him. It was as though she were greeting him, or making some casual pleasantry in the street. She smiled, and it was that smile that was to remain with him, taunting him, mocking his confusion as he drove out through the messy suburban sprawl of south London towards Rawley.

Daniel shut himself up inside the house, a glass of whisky never very far away from reach, robbed of any real desire for movement. Names and faces entered the house at will; they stalked the corridors and the rooms with complete freedom. Since the destruction of the library it was ridiculous to pretend that he was safe, or that Rawley offered a refuge from the world outside. Yet there was a grim irony in it all, for whereas he felt he was never alone, that Edgar and even Abel mixed freely with the fainter shades of George Hutchinson and his father, he was quite incapable of reaching people when he needed them. Abel. Helga. Jenny, and even Arthur. All of them elusive, apparently impossible to know, beyond all hope of contact. Rawley, and the world outside Rawley had suddenly turned a different face, and proved, in spite of the illusion of warmth, in spite of the talk and the awesome promise of physical contact, to be cold and very lonely places.

He waited without purpose, drifting from room to room, staring for hours at a time at the thick grass of the field outside, and thinking of the offensive yellow and red brick of the wretched little estate that Perkins had put up over the rise. Parklands. A small community living in bungalows with foundations that barely scratched the topsoil. Not that he held any blame over the heads of those men and women who lived in Parklands. Far from it. The village of Rawley had come a long way since the fifties. Nearly three thousand people now, with its regular commuter trains, its public services, its clean sanitary air and, thank God, as everybody said, its green belt and building codes and God only knew what else to keep everybody safe from the world outside. He didn't blame them, he told himself. Rawley was theirs. Theirs to inherit. The earth. The Wealden clay. The thousands of years of men looking south towards the sheep-crossed Downs and the Channel beyond. The small Saxon church – St Wilfred had been there – and the old duck pond. All theirs. Yes, there was still a beauty to Rawley, still the suggestion of an old Sussex village that clambered up and down its little bit of hill, with its God and His house, and those Victorian parvenus, the Rosses, with their unsightly manse (his home, with its memories and ghosts, its rusted drainpipes, and its notebooks filled in the thin scrawl of Edward Ross, dead at Meerut). No, he had no hate for these good men and women of England, these silent, complacent inheritors of this ancient place. He bid them welcome, settle, take, and fill the sod with their bones.

Perkins. A rich man now. Change a little here, add a bit there and you wouldn't know him from a man whose history in the middle classes went back five hundred years. He knew he should dislike Perkins. It was not just the drink that told him that. He should hate him because of what he'd done. But there was the rub. There was a bond between them, a subtle fibrous bond, an invisible cartilage that pulled them together. It was not just that Julie stood between them, though they'd talk about her often enough. Perkins probing, pathetically trying to extract scraps of information about her, desperate just for the sound of her name. It was more the dull, unspoken affection. And there was too much of the old Viking in him, too much of the animal rapacity that had brought wealth into his own family, for Daniel to condemn. To condemn Perkins would be to condemn his own line, his own blood.

The days passed, one drifting casually into the next. Polly brought him food. She took his drinking with an easy calm; she'd learnt to accept the existence of far less certain things in life than this occasional drunkenness of his. She watched him from corners and doorways and at times, he fancied, even sat beside him. Yet there was nothing desperate in this drinking. He never felt that he had lost control. He wanted to drink because he was frightened by the pace of his reactions. He wanted not to kill his senses, but to dull them so that later he might live; he craved life.

It was a Sunday when he broke the pattern and went out into the village for the first time. He parked his car outside the church; he liked St Wilfred's. It lay in the centre of the village, small, with its neat little cemetery set off from the road by a wych gate. The congregation had swollen immensely since the days of his family's participation in parish affairs, and he watched with interest as the matrons of Parklands spilled out of the church with their husbands and children in tow. This was a decorous scene. A sunny, if not warm day. Early summer. In the hedgerows beyond Rawley he knew there would be thick crops of primroses and rushes of violets. Up in the woods there'd be bluebells. There were memories in all of this, and these people in their Sunday best, their hats, their suits, the children in their long white socks and brown and black shoes, spilled over into them. They came out of St Wilfred's, serious-faced, turning here and there to each other, to point, to nod, and pass on. In the lane outside the cars started up. Modern cars, all of them no more than a year or so old.

Last of all, in a tight bunch of men and thick-ankled women, came Perkins, sober in a black suit, strutting like a bantam. Seeing Daniel he came immediately across, stood for a moment outside the car door, then opened it and sat down.

'Let's drive, then,' he said.

Daniel felt apprehensive about his sitting there, felt him taut and in the mood for a fight, which was why he turned off the old lane that led out of Rawley and into the right-angle of concrete that so crudely connected the old village with the new estate.

He drove slowly, passing the parked cars which had just come down from the church, and systematically went up and down the roads of the estate, pausing here and there to stare at an open stretch of grass, a dog squatting on a lawn, a pram left untended outside a front door.

'It's not Parklands we need to talk about,' Perkins said, 'so don't try getting me all riled up about it.'

'What's up, Walter?'

'You know damn well what it is.'

They drove over to the Fox and Hare in silence. A small pub, but usually full on a Sunday. Couples up from the coast or down from the southern suburbs. Rawley had its own small band of devotees.

Perkins took a corner by the fire, put his half pint down on the table, and said, 'So you let her do it.'

Daniel nodded. 'That's what she wanted.'

'And you're happy now, I suppose. Shot of it for good.'

'There's no other way.'

'That's a lot of cock, Dan, and you ought to know it. You don't go giving in like that.'

His face was screwed up, intent. Red blotches marked his cheeks. His blue eyes were slightly faint. Walter Perkins was not the type to give in easily.

'I didn't think you cared particularly,' Daniel said, though he knew the cut was unkind and unjustified.

'Why? Because I left it to you and didn't go barging in when I wasn't wanted? Of course I cared. She's my daughter.'

'More than she was ever my wife.'

'That's as may be, but then you'd be the one to blame for that. Nothing but what a firm hand wouldn't have settled.'

'For what? I can see now that there was never a marriage in it, Walter.'

'More than there will be with that cocksucker.'

Daniel laughed, amused at the man's tenacity, but then stopped suddenly, largely because he was struck for the first time that Julie's father had suddenly begun to show his age. The aggression was still there, the posing, the face, but the energy and the bite had gone out of it.

'Charles is what she needs,' Daniel continued. 'A good, successful, professional man.'

Perkins shook his head. 'I never liked the man. Couldn't see what your father saw in him either. Then your father was no real judge of men.' For a moment his eyes lit up and he grabbed Daniel's arm. 'I never told you about the time your father came over and cornered me. "Perkins," he said, "Perkins, I'm interested in selling out."'

Daniel tried to imagine his father going across like that. It seemed improbable. Impossible. It hadn't been his father's style. He would have had an agent do it for him. He smiled. It was rare that he caught Perkins out in a deliberate lie; this time there seemed so little point in it.

'Hard-headed,' Perkins said. 'That was Julie's problem. Always running around like a tomboy. I tell you, it was no joke bringing her up without a woman in the house.' Daniel waited as Perkins paused. 'When she was twelve she began to change. It happened. You know. The way they change.' The words dried up on him and Daniel knew that yet again Perkins had been led on by appearances and his money into an easiness in which he had finally confused himself. In the end this was what always happened. Words were a barrier, a series of obstacles with which he was always in violent collision. But he would never give in, never admit his defeat. Seconds later he tried again. 'I watched her, knowing I should say something, but it wasn't until a year later that I managed to get her to stand still long enough while I tried to explain. Me, of all people.' He laughed, then almost drained his half pint in a single draught. Putting the glass down noisily he said, 'The silly bitch laughed in my face.'

'Julie thinks the world of you,' Daniel said.

He nodded. 'It may be.'

'I shouldn't worry about them. You'll get used to the idea.'

'I doubt it. He's not the kind of man I could ever get to like somehow.'

Daniel knew what he meant. There was an unmistakable condescension in Charles Ponting towards those whom he didn't consider his social equals. It was obviously something he was aware of and which at times he tried to hide, but there was no hiding it from a man like Perkins who'd spent so much of his life tolerating condescension in the course of his daily work. And with Julie he doubted that it would make much difference. Julie would never have admitted feeling awkward about her father, but Daniel knew she would not try to fight Ponting's covert distaste. After a time they'd begin to laugh at him. Develop small family jokes. Perkins was no fool; he could see it coming and it was difficult to blame him for reacting as he did.

'A hard hand is what she needed and I never gave it to her. Always having her own way. Flaunting herself.' He looked at

Daniel archly and laughed. 'Oh, don't think I don't know about the way she used to go to the woods and air her fanny for every Tom, Dick and Harry to have his eyeful. Brazen bitch. Should have whipped her.' He grabbed Daniel's arm. 'You should have whipped her.'

Daniel laughed aloud. The thought of his actually taking a whip to Julie seemed absurdly funny. Until he remembered Jenny.

'And what good did all that education do her?' Perkins continued, following an old vein.

'She's got what she wanted.'

Perkins finished off the few drops in his glass and ordered another round. 'She doesn't know what she wants, and never did too. None of them do, that's the bloody trouble.' He fretted in his seat. Picked at a plate of crisps. Eased around his collar. 'Bloody women. Nothing but bloody moan. What did it do for her, anyway? Married to a posh snot like Ponting, washing his dishes and playing games with all his fancy friends.'

'You're forgetting she's got a mind of her own, Walter.'

'No, I'm not at all. There's some things you don't forget.'

'She'll very likely continue her career and he'll be able to help her. Besides, these days women do all kinds of things. In Russia . . .'

'Fuck Russia.'

Daniel dropped the subject and said, 'Julie and I made a mistake. Or at least I made the mistake.'

'That's not the way you used to talk. You used to hold that marriage was forever. Sounded like a preacher.'

'I've learnt a few things since then.'

He nodded, and then there followed a silence of a few minutes, one of those many silences they'd fall into but which neither of them had really learnt how to handle. It was as though Perkins had vanished completely inside himself. Words. Vigour. Prejudices. The lot. The pub had filled up while they'd been talking, a Sunday morning crowd with a mixture of accents and professions. This was the new Rawley. New money. New hairstyles. Majorca in the summer, perhaps something more adventurous for a few, like Casablanca or Hammamet. Young kids too, Daniel noticed, who couldn't have been more than sixteen at most. Smiling. And the knowledge and tiredness that comes with a virginity long gone.

'So you took a fancy elsewhere,' Perkins said.

Daniel looked up in surprise.

'With her.' He nodded towards the door. 'The wife of that man.'

This was Walter Perkins at his most obscure, but the language was rich enough, with the stress giving all the real information. Jenny. His views. The fact that it was common gossip.

'Who's been talking to you?' Daniel asked.

But he wouldn't be drawn. 'Skinny bit,' he said, sucking his teeth. For a moment Daniel was unsure of him and wondered if he was purposefully trying to antagonise him.

'You're wrong, Walter.'

'Bullshit. You've been that road, boy.'

'No, you might not believe it, but I've remained completely faithful to your daughter.'

'Then you're as daft as the rest of the Rosses.' He grinned, then said, 'I'm not riled at you. It's a free country.'

It was only then that Daniel realised that Perkins was upset not just because of the impending divorce but because he could see their own friendship breaking up. Perkins had few friends; acquaintances he had by the score, but there was more to their relationship than just the odd word and the odd pint. Daniel was sure of it as Perkins looked at him. There was a menacing aggressiveness in the way he followed him with his eyes, but it was more the aggression of a man who was hurt and frightened than of one who wished to cause harm.

'I won't be leaving the area,' he said.

'More fool you. Would be the best thing you could do. There's bugger all here to keep you, except that rotting pile of stones up there on the hill.'

'Nothing to go for,' Daniel said.

'No. There never was with you, was there?'

'Perhaps not.'

'You could have had the world, Dan. You could have had the bloody world. If I'd had half your education I'd have been another Getty. Nothing would have stopped me.'

'If you'd had half my education, Walter, you wouldn't have lifted a finger.'

Perkins grinned and then broke into a splutter of laughter. 'So, you won't be wanting to chase after that other woman, then? No more thoughts of marriage.'

Daniel thought of the way she'd tensed up as he'd touched her, and the look of panic that had swept across her face before she had recovered to deliver that final, masterful comment: Don't be hurt.

'Arthur Hallowes is my friend,' he said.

'He's a strange bird.'

'He is. But I like him.'

'Oh, I don't know why not. You like his wife well enough.'

Perkins turned away, as if regretting what he'd said. Daniel stared at him and then stood up.

'I didn't mean anything by that, Dan.'

Daniel nodded. The smoke, the dull echo of dribs of talk, the push of cheap cloth, the sweet smell of drink and bodies, enveloped him as he made for the door. Perkins's voice came out from the middle of it all, calling his name. Daniel pushed to the door and hesitated briefly in the sunlight.

Perkins came up to him and tugged at his sleeve, now no more than a small ingratiating dwarf. Sweat stood out on his brow. His lips were thin, pale. His hand rested on Daniel's sleeve, not far from his wrist.

'You'll see Julie again?'

'That would be up to her. I suppose so.'

Perkins eyes searched his, hungrily. 'Busy, I expect. With her job. And him.' He nodded to himself as if satisfied by his own explanation.

By this time they were outside and Daniel was already feeling in his pockets for the car keys when he noticed Perkins stiffen slightly. Following his gaze he turned and saw Jenny standing just a few feet to one side of them.

'Daniel?' A slight hesitation preceded the step she took towards them. Beside him Perkins mumbled inaudibly, then turned and marched off. Without seeing it Daniel knew the set of his face; a mask, blank, the eyes on the road fifteen or twenty feet in front of him. Perkins's comment on Jenny echoed back at him. The wife of that man. David and Uriah the Hittite. That would have been an image for Perkins to play with, in the same way that the Bible with its simple and stark portrayals of right and wrong had played such a part in assuaging the guilt of so many earlier Rosses.

Jenny stopped in front of him. Daniel looked around. Just to one side of them the open doorway of the pub showed vague shapes moving within. The roadway was clear. There was a smell of cleanness in the air. But in the other direction Perkins had stopped and turned around. As Daniel looked towards him Perkins lifted his right hand to the level of his shoulder. A gesture. Complicity, perhaps. But also, perhaps, disgust.

They stood awkwardly facing each other.

'How did you come?' he asked.

'The ten-thirty out of Victoria.'

The engine turned slowly as he tried to start it, and Daniel cursed as he remembered that the battery had been charging poorly. 'The damn thing needs changing,' he said, glad of the distraction.

Beside him, her hands folded neatly in her lap, Jenny said, 'Polly mentioned that you might be down here.'

'You walked up to Rawley?'

'Why not? You live like a king out here. London seems so far away.'

He thought of the walk up from the station. Three-quarters of a mile of slow hill, the small lane narrowing badly at the top but for its full length bordered by thick hedge and giving way at the very crest to a tangle of beech and oak. Sussex oak.

The car turned into the lane that led up to the house. From this distance there was never an occasion when there wasn't something breathless about Rawley. The house was too far away to be seen clearly. Its colour, the grey dark stone, and its sheer size were full of impressions, suggestions. The eye was not killed by detail.

'Jenny, I want to explain about the other day. It's been on my mind. And I didn't know how I was going to see you. Or if you'd come.'

But she wouldn't answer him until they were inside the house.

Jenny had always been very circumspect about Polly, as though she were frightened of her. Polly took her coat, grunted when Jenny said that she appeared to be very fit, and then disappeared towards the kitchen.

'Did I say something wrong?' Jenny asked brightly, indicating Polly's retreating figure. Daniel noticed her smile, and the obvious attempt at gaiety. She didn't want to talk, he told himself. She'd come but she didn't want to talk.

'You shouldn't ever mention Polly's health. She thinks people who do that are secretly trying to work some kind of spell. You know, magic.'

Jenny burst into laughter, and was still laughing when they sat down by the fire in the living-room. Early summer. A winter's fire. Daniel looked into it and thought of Julie sitting opposite him during those early years.

'Julie and I are getting divorced,' he said.

She stared at him open-eyed. Not out of surprise, he knew. It was almost as though she had assumed a mask. Her face told him nothing. In the end she settled back in the chair and said, 'Yes, I heard that.'

'I thought you ought to know.'

'But it doesn't alter us,' she said quickly.

'Jenny, that day when I saw you there like that. What he'd done. I wanted to make you know . . .'

'No. Not like this, Daniel. We mustn't talk about ourselves.' She looked at him, again smiling, only this time it was obvious that the gaiety was forced. 'Never. It wouldn't work.'

'I want to be honest with you,' he said.

Her face clouded and her hands fidgeted on her skirt. She shook her head violently. 'I thought we'd agreed not to talk like this, hadn't we? Because of the way it clouds everything over. I don't want that to happen, please. I can't deal with it.'

He didn't understand. 'But it was you,' he protested. 'It was you who showed me.'

'I was upset. I didn't know what I was doing. I'm sorry.'

'You're trying to hide yourself from what's really happening, Jenny.'

She gasped. 'You, of all people. It's you that has absolutely no idea of what's really happening.' The quickness of the rebuke stung him. She stood up, agitated.

'At least tell me about Arthur. I need to know.'

She shook her head emphatically. 'It's not your business what happens between Arthur and me. Please. I don't want to explain.'

'My God, Jenny, I don't understand you. I've known the man for years and now I find out that I don't know anything. For my sake please tell me. Has he beaten you before?'

'Arthur and I have our own relationship,' she said firmly. 'There are things you wouldn't understand.'

'Why the mystery? Don't I have some kind of claim on you?' He looked at her, small, compact, completely out of his reach. He remembered the urge that had made him go across the room to her the other day when he'd visited her in Putney. It had been out of his control; he had been compelled to go to her, compelled to touch her. He had wanted, in spite of the bruises on her flesh, to possess her. Almost with panic he realised that he had the same feeling now.

He stood up and walked quickly across to the drinks trolley. 'But why Arthur?' With his glass in one hand he asked, 'How could he have done that?'

'Why not? You think he's some kind of god?'

'You can't love him,' he said, turning on her.

'Perhaps not. But I still need him.'

'It's dishonest,' he insisted.

'He loves me,' she said quietly. 'In spite of the evidence. But there are things you don't know about us.'

He offered her a drink, and when she declined took his whisky back with him to his chair. 'And what about Arthur's concern for Abel?'

'So?' She shrugged her shoulders.

'Davison said something about Arthur writing to him all the time.'

She snorted, and without her having to tell him he knew her disgust was levelled at Davison. Then she surprised him by looking up and saying, 'You hardly live in this world, Daniel. God only knows what you see. You wouldn't know the truth even if it were paraded in front of your eyes.'

He thought about the comment, then shook it off. 'I have to see Abel,' he said.

Later, she said, 'Arthur lives in fear of Abel. Abel and his friends. It's madness, of course, but it's how he feels. And that's what his books are all about. Fear of the modern world. Of modern technology. Because Arthur sets himself up as the High Priest representing the old values. Rational man in harmonic balance with nature. Long evenings spent pondering over other men's thoughts. Like you, in many ways, and perhaps in some ways like me too. Things we value highly. Books. The written word. The gift of speech. The freedom to speak our minds, and the time to indulge all our likes and even dislikes. But Abel is different. Articulate in ways we can't appreciate, that's what I tell Arthur. But no, he insists that he's simply an agent of destruction. He doesn't see the possibility of anything else.' She raised her hands as if to explain yet more. 'That's how he feels. Abel terrifies him. He's become a complete obsession. He can't get him out of his head, even at night. God, he even has dreams about him. But then there's also a fair element of the Messiah in Arthur. He wants to save, to bring the damned back from the brink of perdition, etc.' The sudden offhandedness was accompanied by a change in her manner. She lit a cigarette. Her face became alive, mobile, and he felt the effort to include him.

She felt safe, he told himself. Safe from him. The moment had passed and she'd dealt with it perfectly.

'How do you mean?' he asked.

'The way they argue. Talk. Discuss. Arthur flaunting the classics, the world of Greece and Rome, of Caxton and Gutenberg. The master printers. The engravers. And Abel scornful of it all. The books. The endless chattering of fools, as he calls it. Saying, who knows, perhaps quite rightly, that in the end the measure of culture is a true understanding of what you do, and not merely an understanding of what is done or has been done by others.'

Daniel listened uneasily, but it was not so much the content of the discussions between Arthur and his brother which bothered him as it was the fact that they were able to talk at all. At least there was contact. Arthur and Abel. Bob Davison and Abel. But with himself, nothing.

'I suppose you know that Abel and I never really had that kind of relationship. Things weren't so easy between us.'

She watched him make the confession without any show of concern. 'You know that Arthur holds you responsible?'

'For what happened to Abel?'

'Yes. He blames you. Silly, of course.'

Daniel slumped in his seat. It was ridiculous, and yet the idea triggered something in his mind that took a few seconds to come together. When it did he sat up and worked it out slowly. The blame was being put on to him, and if by someone like Arthur then why not by other people too? Edgar, for instance. It made sense.

With some difficulty he went back to the occasion when he had come across Edgar in the library, and having got Jenny's attention went through in detail the events that had led up to the destruction of the books.

She listened attentively throughout. But it was only when he first mentioned the act of vandalism that she started to blanch. He noticed that she turned away from him, as if trying to hide her reactions, but there was no doubt at all that she appeared frightened. Her face had turned pale. Her hands were balled up.

'You've no proof it was him,' she said at last.

'Not absolute proof, no. But it makes some kind of sense.'

'No.' She shook her head.

He watched her, confused by her insistence. 'But you don't even know him,' he said.

She looked up quickly. 'No, of course not. Of course I don't know him.'

She remained in silence after that. He offered to take her out to dinner but she declined. It was as though she had gone into shock. It was only as he went for her coat that she said, 'I think Arthur knows where Abel is. In fact, I'm sure of it. But he won't tell me.'

Arthur Hallowes lived near Rawley in a small hamlet called Three Mills. It was typical Sussex, except that, as with all of the area around Rawley, the Downs could only be seen on the clearest of days. Three Mills was Sussex of the Weald, and in this particular case a low-lying, wet, clayey bit of land that was crossed by a fast stream and dotted here and there by dense patches of beech and oak. For the rest of it there were lanes and hedgerows following sudden ups and downs, quick hills and steep fields of couch grass and cowdung that had all been bypassed by the developer. From a few places near by the gasometers just outside Rawley could be seen, and beyond, the sharp spires of churches that had been built for the most part in the first three centuries of the millennium. It was unprepossessing countryside; wet, without aspect, and self-contained.

Three Mills was a collection of half a dozen cottages and a farm, and Arthur's Mill House. The Mill House was set beside the stream, part wood, part stone and brick. Odd corners of it had been in existence since *Domesday*, but apart from its age there was little to recommend it. Arthur took a somewhat morbid interest in its lack of comfort, and seemed determined to keep the old place in an eternal state of gradual decay because on several occasions he had been offered a considerable sum of money by property developers wishing to turn it into the kind of home they thought would attract money. Ironically, Arthur had money but wasn't interested. The Mill House was his own little bit of England, and he liked it the way it was: wet, troubled by rot, and a little uneven, like the countryside around it, in its structure.

The door was open as usual. In the kitchen – and Arthur insisted that the house be entered through the kitchen – Daniel was greeted by the mongrel and the two cats that lived with him. Arthur himself was standing in front of the sink with an apron tied around his waist and rubber gloves on his hands.

'I was wondering when you'd come,' he said.

Daniel patted the dog and watched as Arthur pulled off the gloves and indicated the teapot on the corner of the table. 'Tea's fresh,' he said. 'Help yourself.'

He then set about replacing the few bits of china that were neatly stacked up beside him on the draining-board. A cup. Its saucer. A couple of plates. A few pieces of cutlery. A large milk jug, with a view of Rye on the side. He was wearing a thick and very loose sweater, above which could be seen the checked trim of his shirt collar.

'I expect you've seen Jenny,' he said easily.

The directness took Daniel by surprise. 'Not for a few days,' he replied warily.

Arthur reached for the teapot and placed a mug in front of him on the table. As he sat down Daniel noticed that his sleeves had dropped into the dishwater. 'She told you?' Daniel asked.

Arthur nodded. Arthur's hands gripped the mug tightly, the only suggestion that he was under any tension. His fingers were massive, the knuckles great joints edged about by rills of flesh.

'I tried to stop myself from going to her,' Arthur said. 'But I couldn't keep away.'

Daniel was embarrassed. It was as though he were talking to a stranger.

'I'm sorry about the whole mess,' Daniel said. 'I came to apologise.'

Arthur looked him up and down before saying, 'It wasn't anything to do with you.'

Daniel reached for a cigarette. 'But I was involved too. You think it all Jenny's fault?'

'It wasn't anything to do with you. I've known about you and Jenny all the time. I knew about it and I've long since stopped worrying about it. It didn't need Julie to tell me for me to know that.'

'My God,' Daniel slumped in the chair. Then he laughed. 'I didn't think you'd believe it. Nobody else seemed to.'

Arthur shrugged his shoulders. 'Gossip. It never worried me. Besides, I knew that with Jenny . . .' he stopped, then reached across the table for one of Daniel's cigarettes.

Much freer in mind now than he had been for some time, Daniel said, 'I thought it would be much rougher than this. One way and another I was getting quite paranoid about you.'

Arthur was standing in the doorway, the mug of tea in his hand. When he finally turned round and moved away from the door Daniel was struck by the intensity of the light outside. A rough lawn fell away from the door towards the stream. As he watched a duck ambled past, turned, and then waddled down towards the water. 'I can't explain about Jenny,' he said. 'I can't explain about the way things are between us and I can't explain the anger that made me treat her the way I did. I'm not looking for excuses; I'm not making any, either. You've got to understand too that what happened between you and her is none of my business. I don't keep Jenny on the end of a leash; I couldn't, even if I tried.'

It was only then Daniel became really aware of the full power of Arthur's will. He felt it as a blind powerful force emanating from every inch of his body, an aura so intense that it precluded any contact initiated from the outside. Its nature was entirely protective, isolating him from anyone who threatened to come too close.

'What about Abel?' Daniel asked.

Arthur walked outside and Daniel followed. Some ten yards away down the stream there were the remains of an old building, rotten timbers and a huge rectangle of stones and chips of mortar and flint, which had once been connected with the water-wheel that still sat askew in the path of the stream. 'Abel,' he said quietly. 'I'm obsessed by Abel. Not just him, but with them all.' He sat down and it struck Daniel that Arthur had been waiting for him to come, had known what to expect and had had the time to choose what he wanted to say. Now it was as though the setting had been specially chosen. Looking more carefully about him he saw with some amusement that there was much in the nature of their immediate surroundings – the house itself, the water-wheel, the quietness of the fields beyond, the absence of any indication of the twentieth century – that spoke not only of the past but also of a form of popularised idea of the past. The kind of memories etched on cheap pictures and biscuit tins, that were part denatured Constable and part pure myth. But after the amusement, Daniel also began to suspect that Arthur had set it up as a form of common ground between them. They both saw themselves as products of the old ways and traditions. They both believed in the supremacy of man, and that it was his ability to reason that made him better than the animals. They abhorred force. They were elitists who believed that some men were better than others, that man had to be described in terms of quality, otherwise just what was the purpose of living at all? And yet they believed also in the ability of men to improve, and because of this they respected knowledge and the means by which knowledge was passed from one generation to another, and from one man to another. They believed in books. They believed in the written word. Self-consciously, Arthur had once referred to himself as one of the last heirs of the master printers.

'Everything about him obsesses me, Dan. His rejection of you. Of Rawley. The world that you and I know. I get the impression that Abel has no faith in time. The past means nothing and he doesn't believe in the future. If you listen to Abel and his friends talking you'll see that they desecrate the future by filling it with science fiction heroes and improbable, irrelevant fantasies. Not that they see that these fantasies are cheap. They don't see that what they're doing is rejecting the entire process of civilisation. Their heroes have non-human forms, non-human emotions, non-human minds. The same too with their language, their deliberate escape from precision, from exact meaning. Their love of vague generalities, of slang so meaningless and temporary in its reference that in many ways it's little different to the grunts and cackles made by a family of chimpanzees. They don't use language to communicate ideas, because ideas are built on faith, but to communicate feelings, a sense of community perhaps, but at any rate an animal thing. And with Abel, language is also a means of cutting himself off, of exclusion, of self-identification. I even dream about Abel. Sometimes so terrifying that I wake up, sweating. Jenny and I used to talk about it. Mostly she'd laugh and say I was crazy, or making myself crazy. We still talk about it.' He stopped and pushed his large hands through the grass. There was enormous energy in his voice, which lay heavily over this temporary silence, and Daniel found it a relief when he continued. 'You see, I still believe in words. I have to. I have to try to reach him.' Then in a different tone he said, 'One night I dreamt of the end of Rawley. I dreamt that Abel bought it up, but you didn't know that he was the buyer. And then I dreamt that he took it down, stone by stone, and had it boxed up and sent to America. There it was re-erected, in Arizona or New Mexico or some other such place, and filled with collections of what many people associate with England. Pub signs. A small tea shop. Old copper kettles and bedpans. Pictures of kings and queens. Clothes from Marks and Spencers and Kensington Market. Models of famous castles. A copy of the Magna Carta. Replicas of the axes that killed Raleigh and Mary Queen of Scots. Images in wax of figures out of Dickens. Mr Micawber. Tiny Tim. Little Dorrit. Pip. Uriah Heep. And wax figures too of Winston Churchill, Shakespeare and William Wordsworth. The rooms and corridors of Rawley were filled with junk. The statue of Truth Overcoming Evil had been removed from beneath the cupola and placed on the front lawn, but cunningly remodelled so that water leapt out of Truth's nipples and splashed into an ornamental pond in front. In the place vacated by the statue had been placed a large merry-go-round where the cars were various forms of carriage and conveyance, including the hansom cab, Stevenson's steam locomotive, the Spitfire and Concorde. And people came to see all this. Rawley was full of tourists, photographing the place from every angle. They photographed Winston Churchill and Mr Micawber. They photographed Truth's nipples. They photographed lacy bras and panties with the St Michael tab displayed on the back. And outside, standing at the gate, your brother Abel, collecting the dollar entrance fee.'

Daniel was staggered by the absurdity of it all. Abel was

different, that was indisputable. But he saw no reason at all for the kind of preoccupation that had so taken over Arthur. Until he remembered Edgar and the library. The senselessness behind that act of destruction had continued to worry him, and yet, however much he tried to explain it to himself, he still remained confused. Arthur, Jenny had told him, held him to blame for what had happened to Abel. And if that were the case then presumably Edgar felt the same way. Yet that alone was insufficient reason for what had happened. A mere matter of loyalty or friendship would never have occasioned such violence.

'Jenny said that you hold me to blame for what happened to Abel,' Daniel said.

'Nonsense.' Arthur blinked, then shook his head in continued denial. 'Of course I don't hold you to blame.'

'And Edgar?'

Arthur pulled himself to his feet and walked down to the edge of the stream. 'I didn't know you knew him,' he said.

'I want to know about Edgar.'

Arthur thought for a while before saying, 'I don't know whether it's fear or respect, but he has a grip on them all. With Abel there's still some means of communication, but not with Edgar. There's something terrifying about him. There's a violence in him, a lack of patience, an arrogance of opinion that belongs to another world altogether.' He stopped and said, 'How did you meet him?'

Daniel thought of recounting what had happened, but decided against it. 'I heard about him,' he said offhandedly. Then, following on from what Arthur had just said he asked, 'How do you mean that he has a grip on them?'

'Because he's strong-willed. He knows what he likes and what he dislikes, and perhaps that's something people like Abel need, what they crave for.'

'There's nothing political in it?'

'Yes and no, depending on where you draw your boundaries. But I do know that Edgar works at a very basic level of human emotion. I've tried to talk to Abel about this, but even if he does really understand what's going on he doesn't seem able to explain. This is what I was trying to say earlier. It's as though he's lost all faith in words. I don't know what he wants, and he can't tell me. The only thing I can get out of him at all is a vague idea of things they don't want. There's a sense of disgust. A sense of reaction. But it's all on the level of feeling. I don't understand it because they won't give me the words; they won't and probably can't say.'

'Is Edgar capable of physical violence?'

'Yes. I think so. In fact I'm certain of it. But we've been through this before, Dan. You know it's something I've been trying to say for years. Not that people would listen. They don't want to listen; they don't want to know. There's been an air of complacency for too long now, the sort of thing that is left when the real spirit behind Dunkirk and the Battle of Britain disappears and all you've got left is cant, and the emptiness that exists when people mistake cant for sincerity. This country is in for years of violence, and believe me it's only just started. I guarantee it in factories, at social events and in the political system. You ask if Edgar is capable of violence and I have to say yes, because he is a product of a gradual degeneration in our mentality, and because people either don't care to see what they're doing or what is being done, or because they've lost the ability to see it. I'm not exaggerating when I say he terrifies me. He terrifies me because I can't stop him. I don't want the particular values which I feel important to be washed away, but I look around, Dan, and it's obvious to me that you and I are living at a time when what we have to say just isn't being listened to anymore. Things are changing, and Edgar and people like him are the agents of change. There's a frightening lack of recognisable human feeling in them, but then perhaps we're wrong in looking to them for a valid alternative. They have no alternative to offer. All they're saying is that our beliefs and the manner in which we practise them are no longer acceptable, and that's justification enough. They'll fight us, these people. Over the years there'll be more and more violence. God alone knows what lies ahead. Edgar doesn't know and probably doesn't care. And we don't know either.'

A little later Arthur led the way back to the kitchen, where they sat around the table eating cake. This time Daniel found himself looking around with new interest. The darkness of the rooms.

The coats hanging in the hallway and the smell of damp, of things unmoved, of an almost semi-permanent absence of real daylight. In the living-room it was the same. An upright piano. A grandfather clock with the pendulum hanging quite still in the tall upright case. Yet it hadn't always been this way. When Jenny had been there, in spite of its obvious need for repair, the Mill House was still a bright and pleasant place. The clue, of course, was in her absence. Obviously since her departure little had been done. The rooms had been left to rot quietly, without disturbance. There was dust on the shelves. Even the sweater Arthur was wearing had holes.

'Why did Abel try to kill himself?' Daniel asked.

'Maybe just because he didn't care.'

'About living?'

'Something like that.'

'No, it's too easy. It goes against everything I know about him. He just isn't that kind of person.'

'Then what kind of person is he?'

Daniel watched him across the table as he methodically scooped together the crumbs of the sponge cake before putting them into his mouth.

'You're using the wrong method, Daniel. You want reasons. Logical causes. But you're not going to find them. Abel and Edgar, they're operating under different impulses than the ones you and I understand.' He stopped, then after some hesitation added, 'I wonder if it isn't more widespread than it appears at present. The violence that erupts when reason breaks down, when social form can no longer bear the pressure of ordinary relationships.' He pushed aside the plate and, taking a different tack, said, 'I'm not sure, but I think that someone has been getting at Abel. Using him, feeding him drugs. I've tried to get it out of him, but he won't talk.'

'Then you do know where he is,' Daniel said.

'Yes.' He went in search of a piece of paper, then scribbled down an address. 'I don't know if I've been right or wrong in this,' he continued, 'but I know Lillian pretty well and she'll take good care of him.' As he gave Daniel the address he added, 'I want you to promise me that you won't give Jenny this address. Don't ask why. But for God's sake don't let her know.'

After this Arthur grew restless and frequently looked at his watch. When Daniel asked him if he was getting in the way he denied it heatedly and, although it was still afternoon, pressed him to sit down with a drink. After the second drink Arthur got up and paced the room, before finally stationing himself at the window. This erratic, and for Arthur frantic, activity climaxed in a hurried dash towards the stairs. When he came down again Daniel noticed that he had changed his clothes. It was then too that he saw Jenny standing in the doorway.

Daniel took it all in quickly. Arthur had expected Jenny to come; perhaps, he thought, she came down regularly. They had never talked about Arthur, except obliquely, and he had come to the conclusion that the two of them hardly met. And yet the evidence had always been that Arthur still felt very strongly about his wife. Jenny was never without money, and Daniel recollected that there were times when she would disappear and later, when pressed, would refuse to tell him where she'd been. Now the answer seemed simple. Obviously she'd come down here, to be with Arthur.

Arthur went across to her immediately, fussed over her, took her coat and pushed her through to the living-room. Daniel followed it all, partly with amusement, partly with the sense of guilt that he would often feel about his relationship with Jenny whenever he was around Arthur.

Daniel tried yet again to leave, but both Jenny and Arthur insisted that he stay. It was as though they each wanted him as an observer; as though, he told himself later on, they wanted him to witness a part of their relationship which they had so far kept secret from everyone else. For the first hour he remained, self-conscious, wondering if there was a particular purpose to Jenny's visit, wondering if anything was going to happen. Incredibly, nothing happened. Jenny, it appeared, had brought some food down with her and intended making dinner. She did this casually and without any fuss at all, as though it were something she did every day. After a while Arthur relaxed, and Daniel found himself listening with some envy to the conversational banter between them. They both tried to include him; but he responded uneasily, looking for a trap and surprised to find each time that there appeared not to be one. Finally, just after eight o'clock, Arthur asked Jenny if she intended staying over till the next day. She sat for a time looking at him, then shook her head.

'I'll go back,' she said. 'Perhaps Daniel would run me to the station.'

Once in the car Jenny put her hand on his arm and said, 'He told you, didn't he?'

Daniel had known that he wouldn't be able to keep Abel's address from her if she pushed him. Why Arthur had demanded such secrecy he didn't know, and in some ways the pointlessness of it angered him.

'Yes, but he asked me not to tell you. I don't know why, and I'm not going to ask, but please don't push me to tell you.'

'You're going there now, aren't you?' she said, studying his face. Daniel had drawn up outside the station and was about to open the door so that he could walk her across to the platform.

He nodded. 'Yes. I have to go.'

'Take me up to town?' She smiled broadly and kissed him on the cheek. 'You really surprised me today,' she said. 'You seemed to take my sudden arrival very well.'

When he didn't respond she asked, 'What's her name? The woman Arthur's put your brother up with? You see, I do know something about it.' Daniel continued to remain silent and she said, 'They always fascinate me, these do-gooders. Even you, Daniel. You and your good works. I've never really been able to work it out. Now Norma and her activities I can understand. Norma's forever broody, like an old hen. Still, married to that man I suppose she has to find some outlet for her energies.'

Her hand dropped to his knee.

'Take me there,' she said.

They crossed the river at Putney, but again she insisted. 'I know it's in Islington.' Her voice was strained, and there was a tautness, an eagerness about her that Daniel couldn't understand.

'I promised him I wouldn't tell you,' Daniel said. 'If you respect . . .'

She laughed. 'Daniel, you're outrageous. You come out with the most absurd antiquities. What on earth has this got to do with respecting anything? I'm curious, that's all. I want to see this light out of Arthur's past.'

Helplessly, he drove on through Fulham, then turned north towards Islington. They stopped finally outside a large renovated house, three storeys high and quite obviously suggesting a fair amount of money. 'Lillian,' Daniel said as they sat there in the car. 'Her name's Lillian Feather.'

As they approached the house the door opened wide and Lillian Feather came out to meet them.

She looked at Jenny for a moment, then turned quickly to Daniel. Her face was flushed and her breath short. 'Arthur just phoned,' she said.

'Arthur's been keeping you secret, Lillian,' Jenny said gaily, then added, almost certainly unnecessarily, Daniel thought, 'I'm Jenny.' Lillian appeared in a different light at that first meeting than Daniel was to think of her later on. She seemed much squatter and coarser, and there was an edge to her voice that suggested a lifetime spent within a few miles of the Thames and a minimum quota of a couple of packets of cigarettes a day. There was little of the impressiveness he was to find in her later. On that evening in May he saw only the physical side of her. The weight of the shoulders and the ungainly mohair sweater which hid them, and the bright yellow slacks that clung to her massive thighs. For the rest of her he saw a face that wore lipstick and powder in a seeming attempt at the grotesque, and amazingly fine hands with two rings, one a single diamond, the other a sapphire, on the fingers.

He was struck too by the expense that had obviously gone into decorating the house, or at least what he was then able to see of it. It was not just a matter of money laid out with abandon, but money that had obviously been carefully spent on things which had been carefully chosen. There was not the artiness of Bob

Davison's flat, not the feeling that things had to be lived around, looked at and admired. Everything about the place seemed to have been chosen to blend, to disappear. The carpets, the wallpaper, the furniture and even the paintings on the walls existed as part of each other. There was an overall sense of harmony, of a complete lack of competition.

They were ushered into a small room at the back of the house, presumably quite close to the kitchen for there was the unmistakable smell of vegetables cooking, and a feeling that the humidity was slightly higher as though not too far away there were great amounts of steam and boiling water. Association very readily took him back to the kitchen at Rawley, to Polly and his mother. Jenny, however, was restless, but it was not so much the charged energy that so often filled her and which would more than likely appear on the surface as criticism, as it was a lack of confidence. For one of the very first times since he had known her Jenny appeared nervous, almost frightened.

'So,' Lillian said, looking hard at Jenny. 'I always wondered when I would be allowed to meet you.' For a moment a shadow of extreme hostility passed across her face, but for a few seconds only and later on Daniel was to doubt that he'd seen it. Then Lillian's eyes, which were very round and an extraordinarily rich brown, suddenly opened wide and her whole face burst into a deep smile. 'You know what I used to say to him? "Arthur, why won't you let me meet her? Or is she so special?"' She threw the last word out with a sweep of her right hand. Ash fell across her thighs on to the carpet. 'And never would he show me a photograph. Not once.' Her body fell slightly so that she had to lift her elbow on to the arm of the sofa. The movements were exaggerated and alarming, and Daniel was to learn later that usually she carried her weight around with an enviable grace. Yet there was also an element of the clown in her which occasionally would break through, making her parody the image she visually projected. But she did not need to do it; it was done out of awkwardness, an offering to appease a sudden spurt of restlessness.

'That's unlike Arthur,' Jenny said. Her body was tight. Her hands were clasped around her knees. Her face was drawn.

Lillian continued to look across at Jenny, then nodded. 'And I don't suppose he ever mentioned us up here before,' she said.

Jenny whispered quietly that he hadn't.

'Such a secretive person when he wants to be. Such a wretched man.' Then she looked up in alarm, but it was mock alarm, her face turning from one to the other of them as though she were a small child who had done wrong and now expected reproach.

'However, I don't want to slang poor old Arthur behind his back. The trouble is, of course, that I wouldn't dare do it in front of him. He'd probably throw me out of my own front door. He did that sort of thing too. When we were kids.'

She let it all sink in. She and Arthur had known each other for years. The relationship predated their own separate arrivals. And the fact that Arthur had chosen not to tell them only served to underline what she was trying to say. This was another world, and though they were invited to enter they were being asked to tread very carefully.

'Mrs Feather,' Daniel said, 'Arthur said you knew about Abel. That he's staying here with you.'

She narrowed her eyes. 'I know as much as some. Less than others. And if my husband heard you call me that name he'd probably wet his pants laughing.'

'Abel came here recently?'

'Yes. But he's not here now.'

He felt that she was evading him purposefully, that for some reason of her own she was reluctant to tell him what he wanted to know.

She sat up again and put another cigarette in her mouth. 'How about a drink? Tea? Anything but coffee. It's bad for my heart and I don't keep it in the house. The cigarettes I can't give up.'

She rose from the chair and disappeared out of the door.

Jenny sank back in her seat and whistled quietly. 'God,' she said, 'I could hardly breathe.'

Lillian reappeared carrying a drinks tray. Putting it down she said, 'I don't suppose then that Arthur would have told you anything about what we're trying to do. I suppose you could call it something of a self-help community; nothing to do with the law or what goes on in the state system.' She drew herself up and indicated the walls of the house and the world outside. 'Kids come and go as they like. They know me and the rules I work by. I don't have any qualifications, and nor does my husband. So far as the local authorities are concerned all we're doing is running a boarding house, and except for the way it works that's exactly what it is.' She established herself more comfortably in her chair and said, 'That's by way of a little speech I have to trot out every now and again. People like to know, and I'm only too glad to tell them. Co-operation, that's what I believe in, not handouts.'

The woman's manner took Daniel aback. More than ever he felt that she was attempting to erect a barrier between them, though he could see no reason at all why it should be so. Particularly, he felt her antagonism towards Jenny, though Jenny herself, in spite of her mild protest a minute or so before, seemed to have lost her original nervousness and to have settled down quite comfortably.

'Arthur said that he'd sent Abel here,' he said. 'Do you know where he's gone?'

He felt her eyes cut quickly across his face. 'He'd be out somewhere with those lads he knocks about with. On their bikes, more than likely.'

Edgar. Daniel wondered what she knew about him.

Standing up and with uncharacteristic forwardness he said, 'Then I'd like to go up to his room.'

It was obvious that she was taken aback by the request. She hesitated, then pushing Jenny to one side went out of the door and pointed the way up the stairs.

'You'll find it,' she said, but by the time they had turned around to ask for clearer directions she'd disappeared.

In fact they found the room almost immediately. The door stood ajar, almost as though it had been left open on purpose.

'Something tells me that she didn't want us to come up here,' Daniel said as they went in.

Jenny gave no sign of having heard but sat down almost immediately in a chair and lit a cigarette.

It didn't take long for Daniel to realise that Abel wasn't the sole occupier of the room. 'They're both here,' he said, the surprise quite evident in his voice. 'Both of them.'

Jenny smiled. 'It looks like it.' She stretched her legs and let her eyes wander up to a picture of Helga on the dressing table. Helga in Brighton, seeming even younger than she was, leaning against the railings on the Front. Beside her, Abel. His hair tossed out and blowing up around his head. Behind them a taller figure astride a motorbike at the side of the road. Edgar.

'So, what do you do now, Daniel Ross?' Jenny asked. 'Wait for the return of the prodigal?'

The question disturbed him. 'I don't know.'

'But this is why you came here, isn't it? To talk to him. To lead him back on to the straight and narrow. Daniel, the servant of the Lord, reclaiming the souls of the damned.' She laughed out loud, and he was struck by the sudden but inappropriate levity.

'It's not so easy as that,' he said.

'But you're such a pompous ass, Daniel. Here you are, after God knows how many days of worrying, at the end of the trail. You've found him. The lost sheep is found. It's all over, Daniel.'

She spluttered with laughter and he found himself so embarrassed that he went across to the door and shut it.

After a time he sat down and said, 'But they're still together. She went to look for him.' Then, noticing the cot in the corner behind Jenny he said, 'And they've got the kid with them.'

Jenny spun round and stared at the cot. Quickly she got to her feet and went across to it. For a while her face clouded over, but it soon resumed the gaiety of the previous few minutes. 'I don't think so,' she said. 'It hasn't been used. Besides the child wasn't well enough to be brought into a place like this.'

Irritated by the tone of her voice, he said, 'I don't see you have any right to be so pleased about it. And the truth is I always wanted her to keep the child.'

'Don't be so romantic. Only a fool would dream of bringing up a child under such ridiculous circumstances.'

Her mood confused him, and rather than try to analyse it he determined to ignore her. In an attempt to forget his unease he started to look more closely round the room and saw, this time, that it was full of objects that he had not noticed before. A cross hanging on the wall. A small statue of the Virgin Mary. Cheap mementoes from Fatima and Lourdes. And photographs. Of

Edgar astride his bike. Of Abel and Helga together. Elsewhere in the room a small silk glove, black, draped over the mirror on the far wall. A dressing-gown. A slip with lace around the hem. A jar of coffee on a nearby chair. A wallet, with at least four or five ten-pound notes tucked inside, lying just next to it. A large fluffy rabbit near the cot. A plastic rattle. And on a small table, just to his right, a telegram.

CONGRATULATIONS DARLING ON THE BIRTH OF YOUR BEAUTIFUL SON I LOVE YOU AND HOPE TO SEE YOU SOON MUMMY

Daniel stared at the telegram, then at Jenny who reached out and picked it up.

'Funny,' he said, 'that I never thought of her mother.'

'Funny,' Jenny retorted, 'that her mother never thought of her.' She rolled the telegram into a ball and threw it on to the floor.

Daniel stood up and went across to a large photograph of Edgar which he now saw was pinned to the back of the door.

'That's him,' he said.

Jenny glanced up and then quickly looked away. 'Who?' she said. She tossed her cigarette away, then lit another.

'Edgar. The one I told you about.'

'Just another mixed-up adolescent,' Jenny said. 'There's thousands of them. Wanting attention. Wanting to be loved. The usual, endless crap.'

After a while he said, 'I talked to Arthur.'

Her eyes lit up. 'About what?' She stared hard at him.

'About Edgar.'

'And what did he say?'

It hit him then that she had to know Edgar, in spite of her previous denials. That time when he'd first told her about the destruction of his library she'd suddenly paled, and had acted as if under great strain.

'So you do know him,' he said.

She shook her head, and her defence was fast and biting, 'Don't be ridiculous. How could I?'

But it was not just Jenny who was keeping things from him.

They all were. Arthur. Abel. Even Helga, hiding her religion behind her adolescent indifference and her defensiveness.

'Some day,' he said with a self-deprecating laugh, 'some day somebody is going to tell me what's going on. You. That bloody woman downstairs. Arthur. For the love of God, what's it all about? How about letting me in on the secret?'

She avoided looking at him. 'There's no secret, Daniel.'

'No? Well, who's been pumping drugs into my brother? And why? And why does some lunatic come round and ravage my house? And what about us? After all these years, Jenny, what about you and me?'

He watched her smoke the cigarette, numbed by his own outburst.

'Don't leave me tonight,' he said, as she got up to go.

Her hand reached out, took his and stayed there as he got to his feet.

'We'd better go,' she said.

Outside it was dark. Lillian had not come to the door when they'd left, though Daniel was sure he'd seen a curtain move just as they got into the car. As he put the car into gear he returned to what he'd said just before they'd left the house.

'I don't have any pride left,' he said. 'I'm asking you. Damn it, if you can still go down to Arthur after all the hell he's given you then what about me?'

He felt her subside beside him.

'All right,' she said finally. 'But not my place. A hotel.'

Jenny arranged to meet him in the lobby just after eleven, while he took the opportunity to secure a shaving kit and freshen himself up in the room. He was pleased with the simplicity of the room, though he reflected that under the circumstances he would have been pleased anywhere. He liked the squareness of it; the easy and familiar geometry of it all. The polished wood. The comfortable bed. The unobtrusive painting on the wall. The table lamp sitting squatly on the top of the television. As he paced up and down, knotting and reknotting his tie, he found himself contrasting this room and what it represented – the modern world of fleeting relationships, of impermanent relative values, brief love, its instant music and its television – with the non-mechanical, sturdier, altogether more self-assured if ignorant life led at Rawley. Looking in the mirror he saw himself set like a transfer in the room, an apparently firm and solid object yet so easily removable. With his tie and his conservative clothes, his square-set and not very movable face, he was the image of Rawley, and yet free to come and go as he pleased, even free, he thought, to spend a night or maybe longer in a place such as this.

He ordered wine and a light meal, much to the consternation of the room service. At the initial protestations, the reference to the time and the shortage of staff, Daniel found himself talking as he had rarely done before, whispering encouragements into the telephone and promising that all involved would be well rewarded.

At eleven o'clock, with the wine and the food already laid out in the room, he went down to the lobby to wait. At half-past one he was still there, eyeing the occasional taxi that drove up to the front door, and checking out the passengers that made their way to the desk.

At two o'clock he walked out into the street. The night was cloudy but, incredibly, every now and again it was possible to make out the stars. With a brief and final thought of the untouched meal he walked round to the garage and his car.

The following day Daniel phoned Lillian Feather and asked to speak to Abel. To his surprise he found her much more affable than the previous evening, and she readily gave him an address just south of the river where Abel had set himself up with his friends in a small workshop.

Even before he saw the place he heard the motorcycle. It came to him first as a low rhythmic roar, then changed in tone to an angry clamour. As if tuning in to a long suppressed fear he remembered the bike that Edgar had left by the gate at Rawley, and the photographs of hill-climbs and racing circuits that he'd seen but ignored the previous day in Abel's room. When the bike finally shot out of the workshop entrance, he found himself forced into the unnerving realisation that buried deep within him was a pathological fear of machines. How he had coped with it so far he did not know, but at that moment he was no longer able to doubt that it was the case. Machines, all machines, frightened him. He distrusted their functions; he was overwhelmed by their components; he was dismayed by the expertise and knowledge needed to control them.

The bike passed within inches of him, and it was not until the street was completely silent again that he realised he had stopped moving and his hands were covered with sweat.

The doors opened on to what appeared to him to be an ordinary small workshop. There were a couple of cars inside, one with the engine hauled out and swinging by a hook above the gaping hole beneath the bonnet. The other was without wheels and upholstery. The steering-wheel was completely bent, as though a massive weight had been dropped on it. Although he recognised the makes of the cars he was amazed that the names had completely escaped him. He stared at each one of them, trying to force himself to remember, but without success. Frustrated, not only by this lapse of memory, but also by the seeming absence of people, he went across to a small room that might have served as a general office.

There he was greeted by a mechanic, his overalls covered with grease and paint, who responded to his question by saying, 'You just missed him.'

'He's not here?'

'A minute ago. Maybe a couple.'

There followed a conversation which Daniel dominated entirely. His questions, and the interpretations he was forced to draw in face of the other's silence, nods, and gestures. The further questions he was forced to ask in order to make sure that these interpretations were correct. He discovered that there were about half a dozen people working in the place, and that they all had money in it. He discovered further that it was a general workshop, and that each one of them had separate skills, separate interests. The mechanic pointed outside. Two bikes. Another room full of television sets. Radios. Gadgets and parts that he had never really had to see in terms of their basic components. A television to him had always been an object, something which he could use to entertain himself, perhaps even to educate himself. If forced, he would have described it physically in terms of its outward appearance, the obvious shell and the controls. But these pieces of equipment and the machines which he saw now were alien, devoid of recognisable function, full of nameless parts and unknown relationships. He wandered alone among them. He recognised pieces of printed circuitry, old valves, some transistors and lengths of wiring. But they were all separated from him by his ignorance. Faced with them he was no better than the most primitive of savages.

Yet Abel knew. His hands were informed and could find their way about with ease. They had been taught patterns which Daniel had never dreamt of. He understood relationships that Daniel could not even imagine.

The mechanic looked on absent-mindedly, then disappeared. Daniel's watch told him that it was half-past twelve. Lunch hour.

Telling himself that he would wait for Abel's return, he walked out of the office through a back door and found himself in what he could only think of as a small study. The floor was carpeted. There were two or three armchairs, a table and a small collection of books. On the table, its top stained with oil and ink marks, was an ashtray. In one corner of it stood a bottle of Scotch. In the other a video tape-recorder and a monitor.

Above the table were a few photographs. Half a dozen young men he didn't recognise, three of them on bikes. Then Abel, standing by the railings of Buckingham Palace. And Helga, in the last months of her pregnancy, caught by the camera as she sat at a table reading a magazine. Finally, Edgar. The picture was crudely tacked to the wall by drawing-pins, and as Daniel went closer to examine it more carefully he could see that it had once been crumpled, perhaps even thrown away. The surface was cracked into a hundred different lines and there were tears that ran halfway in towards the centre. Daniel unpinned it carefully, then sat down with the photo in his hand. Edgar was obviously much younger here than he was now. About sixteen or seventeen. He stood awkwardly on a pebbled beach, his hands in his pockets, his body slightly slouched. But the most striking thing was the way he held his head back and away from the camera, as though he resented having his photograph taken. Idly turning the photo over Daniel read: My mother took this picture.

The odd syntax struck him, especially the way it seemed to increase the sense of distance. Edgar. He looked again at the front and wondered why at one time, perhaps in anger, he had thrown this photograph of himself away; why too, later on, he had reclaimed it and pinned it to the wall, with its crude comment there for anyone to see. The truth was that he knew nothing about Edgar. Arthur had his theories, and as Daniel recalled them he remembered the persistence with which Arthur would return to the subject of violence. Yet why should Edgar not be an isolated case, someone it might be possible to dismiss as easily as Jenny had attempted to that day? Except he knew now that Jenny too was frightened of him.

He knew nothing, except that Edgar had taken an interest in him, had walked casually into the house on one occasion, and then later on and without warning broken in and destroyed the most valuable part of it. Why?

Daniel started going through the drawers, pulling out pieces of paper and leafing through files, his fingers working feverishly as though chance alone would give him a satisfactory answer.

How had he known about the books? What instinct had led him there, and not to the few pieces of silver, or the landscapes along the corridor upstairs? It was as if he understood, without having to be told, what would hurt Daniel most. But if Arthur were to be believed then there was more to it than that. The books were only a symbol. It was an entire way of thinking that Edgar was rejecting. And the knowledge and feeling for life that Daniel had grown up with and which he shared with so many of the people in the country he counted as nothing. Worthless.

Abel would tell him. The thought appeased him for a few seconds before he dismissed it as unrealistic. Abel had rejected Rawley, and even now would probably complain at his interference.

His activity ceased. He sat back and looked indifferently at the mess he had caused. Pieces of paper littered the floor. His cigarette had rolled on to the table top and already burnt a scar on the surface. He watched it idly.

When he finally pulled himself together he found that he was drawn to the video. The machine was loaded. The switch was in reach. The actual decision to turn it on was taken almost as an act of defeat. He was out of his depth, and he had no way of knowing how he would ever come back to the surface. As his fingers groped for the switch he recalled the previous evening at the hotel. Jenny, laughing at him. Julie and Ponting, barely tolerating him. And Abel . . . he pressed the switch.

The screen was blurred for the first five seconds, but then the picture brightened. Putney High Street. Daniel stood up, alarmed. It was as though the camera had at one time been mounted on the front of his own car. The same turns in the road. The same familiar landmarks. Until, finally, Jenny's house. The door opened and he waited impatiently for Jenny to appear. But when a figure did appear in the doorway it wasn't Jenny. It was Helga.

He reached forward and switched the machine off. His hands shook lightly as he pushed them away out of sight and into his pockets. With the sudden realisation of what he ought to have guessed a long time ago crowding in on him he made quickly for the door and the street outside.

He drove quickly back to Rawley, much as any wounded animal might take the familiar track back to its den. Jenny and Helga. That was what Arthur couldn't tell him. At one point he laughed aloud. An affair between Arthur's wife and that slut of a girl. Again and again he tried to tell himself that he was wrong, but the proof was too obvious to ignore. Her questioning him about where Helga had gone. Her fear of physical contact. Her trip to the hospital. Arthur's insistence that he keep Lillian's address from her. Not so that she wouldn't meet Abel, but so that she couldn't find Helga. And had Helga at one time tried to get away from her? Presumably. The details he couldn't know. She'd had the affair with Abel. Perhaps Jenny was only a passing figure in the crowds surrounding Helga. Perhaps . . . and then he remembered how Jenny had reacted to his mention of Edgar, and he was certain then that not only did Jenny know Edgar but that she had reason to be frightened of him.

May moved easily into June. Daniel became very jealous of Rawley, reluctant to leave it and confront the outside world. For the first time he found himself understanding Polly Adams' relationship with the house and why she had stayed so long with the family. Yet in the end he was forced to go out, as he knew would happen. The events of the past few months had stirred up a host of complications, none of which had so far been resolved, and although the days passed easily enough there was nevertheless an underlying restlessness, as though the worst were yet to come.

It started with Lillian's letter. The handwriting was large, rounded, and written in irregular spurts across the page. It came on rather cheap scented paper and there was a small design of violets in the top right-hand corner:

> I must see you immediately. Absolutely urgent. Sorry nobody to fix phone. Otherwise would have rung. Please forgive rudeness of note.
>
> Lillian.

Lillian greeted him as though he were someone she'd known for years.

'I see you're alone this time,' she said, and he felt that there was approval in the comment. 'How've you been?'

As he passed into the space just so recently occupied by her own bulk he smelt beer, and it didn't take long to convince himself that her movements were a little unsteady.

'Didn't think you'd come up so quickly,' she said, as she guided him into the same room at the back as he had been led into on the previous occasion. 'Never can tell with some people.' She took her time with her cigarette and then said, 'I don't know why I like you, but there you go.' She let the comment slide, then exhaled a great cloud of smoke. Her eyes opened wide as she smiled at him. Daniel noticed that her hair was already outgrowing its yellow blonde dye. Plastered on top of her head as it was, with the lipstick smeared haphazardly across her lips, she looked like a fat whore. Yet he felt quite safe with her. 'In fact, I used to go with a fellow who looked the very image of you. Clean-cut, not like some of these bloody kids who walk in and out of my door every day, not to mention the nights. The nights! Jesus Christ!' She ended in a splutter of coughing and a sudden gasp for air that seemed to cause her pain. 'And those days weren't so very far away, either. Less than you'd think.'

There was, in spite of her obvious harmlessness, something about Lillian Feather that was close to being obscene. Later he was to know that although it was something she might have naturally fallen into, she had since tended to cultivate it. In everything she did, even in the cumbersome sway of her body, there was the unmistakable sign of intelligence. He was often to wonder if it was not this that attracted him to her, because if she had been merely scheming, which she undoubtedly was, then the combination of guile with physical grossness would have been too ugly to bear. Yet Lillian was to prove quite capable of making an early peace with her would-be detractors. She flattered them, using her own bodily helplessness as a means to build up their egoes. The fact was, of course, that she resented her body. She even resented her lifestyle. The man she had married was a sausage salesman, a quiet balding creature who lived his days in her wake, obedient, domestic, a convenient doormat. Lillian was quick to call attention to his employment, and the physical comparison between them. It was the source of countless jokes, something which she actively appeared to enjoy. The more he was to know her the more he realised that Raymond Feather was totally necessary to her existence. It was as though their marriage was something which she had actively gone out of her way to arrange. She needed the vulgarly humorous comparison in order to extend the joke which she had created out of her own life. Raymond, in fact, had minimised her grossness by becoming part of it. People thought of them as a twosome: Raymond and Lillian, Ray and Lill. They formed a comedy team, but the reality of it was that Lillian was observing it all at a distance, pulling the strings, raising the laughs, and then, when it was least expected, vanishing behind a barrage of words that left people gasping for breath.

'I expect you can tell I've had a drink or two,' she said. 'That's the trouble with beer. Stinks the place out.' She pointed across the room at a bottle of Scotch on a dresser. 'That's all I've got in that line at the moment. How do you want it?'

They went on like that for the next forty-five minutes. She was a past master at a game which he recognised well enough but which she had developed to such an extent that she might just as well have invented it. They talked weather. They talked Spain. Benidorm, in fact, where she'd forced some twenty-odd people to go on tour together. And they talked about the bakery and Mortimer, whom she knew though how she wouldn't say. The topics turned slowly, until after a time he noticed that in a crazy way she was beginning to turn the words in the direction she wanted. Arthur came first. Knowing him as a child. And to prove this she brought out a photograph of the two of them together as children. Again, that was calculated, because the picture said something that would have been almost impossible through the mere use of words.

A country cottage. He imagined that it would have been during or just after the war, and two children. A girl and a boy of about twelve or thirteen. Arthur he recognised, but it was more difficult to persuade himself that this long-legged girl and the woman sitting in front of him were one and the same person. Yet such was the case. On the reverse of the photograph was a message:

> Darling Lily. Arthur and you taken at Rose Cottage, September '43.

In the bottom right-hand corner was scrawled, in another hand, this further message:

To Colonel Harper, this is the photograph of your daughter. Hope it's the one you mean.

She watched him turn the photograph over and then lay it down beside him. Impressions, memories of old conversations with Arthur, all collided to form an uneasy collage. But there was no order. None of it made sense.

'It's about Helga,' she said suddenly. 'Things I thought you should know.'

'If it's about Jenny then I already know.'

Lillian eyed him curiously. 'When did you find out?'

He lied. 'I guessed. After I came here with Jenny that time.'

'You know she's with her then? I mean now.'

He didn't know, but nodded his head nevertheless. A little later he asked, 'And the baby?'

'The baby died.' She spoke directly and kept watching him. 'No use getting sentimental about it. Not now.' Then a little more bitterly she said, 'I suppose you thought it was enough, just paying the bills? You never bothered to go down there. Not once.'

He tensed up at the accusation, knowing it to be true, and remembered the day the child had been born, when he'd gone there and stared for so long into the incubator.

'I wasn't the father,' he said defensively. 'And I didn't know Helga.'

'Perhaps you still don't.' Lillian stretched herself noisily, then said, 'What a bloody mess. You. Your brother. Helga and that woman you brought around here that time. How Arthur ever got himself tangled up with such a scheming bitch I'll never know. She'll ruin Helga. After everything I've tried to do for her . . . God knows why I do try, that's what I think sometimes. You know when I first met Helga? Three years ago. Perhaps two and a half. She was a thin, arrogant, snotty-nosed kid, but I couldn't help liking her. She came in here with a couple of boys one night, screaming and laughing and with language enough to make you want to box her ears. Not that it was anything new to me. The boys brought her here because they knew I'd try to help and not turn her straight over to the police. Which is why I'm not so popular in high places. Not by any manner of means. Talk to the local welfare officers about Lillian Feather and they'll start throwing up. Let them. Bloody high and mighty female messiahs. Anyway, by morning she'd come round a bit and started moping around, crying and sulking. Typical, of course. Sullen, silent. The old story. Eventually I found out her mother's address. Her mother. Dear God. More of a child than her daughter. Liberal, middle class, stinking rich, couldn't keep a man around the house long enough to drive any sense into either her or her children. Still, she's not got a bad thought for anyone, and that's saying something. Butterfly brained. Soft in the head about the sixties and what she calls the sexual revolution and God only knows what kind of rubbish. When I suggested that Helga might stay around with me she leapt at the idea and thought nothing could be better.' Lillian threw up her hands and leant forwards as she said, 'Can you beat that? Christ, what a way for a kid to grow up. Trouble with people like that is that they give everything except the love and affection that's really needed. And that includes kicking them up the backside every once in a while too. So, Helga moved in. Went to school. Played around. Then about three or four months after she'd arrived she really began to develop. It was amazing. Something had happened to her that none of us could work out. She seemed much happier with herself, was much more talkative, and suddenly she was fun. Everybody's favourite, that's what she became.'

'Jenny?' he said, anticipating her.

Lillian nodded. 'Some time after Helga took this turn for the better I found out that she was seeing a lot of this woman. Don't ask me how, but in a place like this you hear just about everything sooner or later. Well, I didn't ask her anything, though perhaps I should have done, and anyway I dare say that the girl wouldn't have told me the truth if I'd pressed her. Then some time later on I went into her room when she was out, and by this time she was out a lot of the time, I can tell you, coming home maybe no more than once or twice a week and never a word of explanation. So, I went in, not because I wanted to poke and pry but because I can't stand filth. Believe me, some of these kids live in it. They're worse than pigs. Anyway, I was going round a bit, cleaning up, dusting here and there and straightening things out, when I noticed the photograph. A woman and a girl. That's all I saw at first. Then I saw that the girl was Helga. As for the other – look for yourself.'

She moved slowly across the room to the mantelpiece and searched around beneath a couple of books and inside an old box before finally pushing her hand behind the clock. When she withdrew it she held the photograph up for him to see. There was no mistaking the face. The aloofness, the distance, the impassivity which was Jenny's special trait and which at times made her so devastatingly beautiful.

'Not a face you'd forget, is it? It wasn't too long afterwards that I learnt who she was. It made sense then, of course, Arthur not wanting her to meet me, although he'd talk about her often enough. Funny, when you think about it, me knowing about Jenny all that time but not being able to work out that she was the woman Helga was seeing. I can tell you that I damn nearly keeled over when you appeared with her that day.'

He continued to stare at the photograph, and it was some time before he realised that Lillian was watching him. He could feel the movement in her face when she said, 'So, I wasn't wrong then. About you and her.'

He didn't reply. Lillian's immediate presence was so overpowering that he felt the words choke before he could give them breath. Avoiding looking across at her he reflected again on the pattern he had been able to build up over the last few weeks. Three years ago Jenny had moved out of the Mill House, and Arthur had agreed to set her up on her own in town. However, every now and again the two of them would meet, and spend time together as man and wife. Then there was himself. The long years of non-physical love between them, or what he had allowed himself to accept as love. Because it was Jenny who had pulled him through those years when his marriage to Julie had been coming apart. It was not Julie with whom he had been obsessed, but Jenny Hallowes. He had worshipped her, and suppressed the physical craving he had for her, the desire to touch and overpower.

'Then Helga left her and started going with Abel,' Lillian continued. 'Quite pathetic, really. Apparently Jenny begged her to come back. Begged to be allowed to come round here to see her. But no. Helga was too smart for that. She'd never told Jenny where she was staying. God alone knows what the reason was, some vestige of propriety left over from her infancy, perhaps. So, Jenny Hallowes never did come here, not even once, in all that time. Until she came with you. She must have been desperate.'

Daniel was worried by the word. There was something desperate in it all. In his own gullibility. In Arthur's acquiescence. In Jenny's own driving obsession.

'And Arthur,' Lillian continued, 'led along from year to year, plodding obediently in whatever path she chose to take. He adored her, of course, and, God help him, still does. I remember him coming here just when he'd first found out, sitting there in that chair. And then accepting it all, agreeing even to her demand for her own place in town. Allowing himself to be up-staged by a sixteen-year-old child, as it turned out. Of course, if Arthur had taken me properly into his confidence then I would have known it was Helga, but he was vague, discreet, God how awfully polite he was, and so understanding it was enough to make you want to throw up. An affair, he said, with a young girl. Something that would pass, he was quite sure of that. But child is the wrong word for Helga. It's her mother who's the child. Helga's totally amoral. A drifter. One minute she's down on her knees gabbling Hail Marys as fast as they'll come and the next time you see her she's doped up to the eyeballs and making lewd suggestions to old men in the park. Then, another day, she'll come up to you and you won't recognise her. Serious. Mature. A woman with a woman's understanding.' Daniel followed her slowly, the conflict inside of him weighing him down.

'I went there one day,' he said. 'To Jenny's place. She was bruised, badly beaten. How could Arthur . . .'

'Yes, I know about that. Not her side, of course. He was drunk. I had him screaming like a lunatic in here, with dear old Raymond, bless his heart, standing in the doorway with his bloody apron still stinking of sausage meat. Well, I got the story from him in the end. He'd found out that Jenny had gone down to the nursing home to see Helga, and while there had persuaded her to abandon the child and go back to live with her. Nice, isn't it? So Helga did abandon the baby, but on the way up to Putney got cold feet and came across to me, sobbing and coughing her heart up. Arthur heard about what had happened, and just for those few hours allowed all the anger and frustration to come to the surface. Frankly I would have gladly killed the bitch, but then I'm not hopelessly in love with her as Arthur appears to be. Even if his critics are wrong about his books he still needs his head examined.'

She subsided in her chair, seemingly collapsed and exhausted. Daniel turned from her uneasily, haunted by the memory of Jenny and his own desire for her, and haunted too by that terrifying sequence on the video screen which had first made him understand what was going on. But why Edgar? The question was one he'd attempted to suppress, hoping, as he had begun to during the previous few weeks' exile at Rawley, that Edgar and his apparent purposeless intrusion would eventually disappear. But looked at now he knew that a cycle had been started which was far from completion. He felt helpless, moved suddenly into a path he was being forced to follow.

'Do you know them all?' he asked.

'Most of them. In and out of here over the past few years. Why?'

'What about Edgar?'

She didn't seem surprised. 'Edgar's different. I've always felt a little frightened of Edgar. It's as though he obeys a code that none of the rest of us can understand. Arthur, mind you, takes things a bit far, I think. Though I do know that Edgar's done some pretty crazy things, and if pushed . . .' She looked up. 'Why him?'

'Who is he?'

She was obviously taken aback. 'You don't know?' She stood up and looked around for her glass. 'Edgar's her brother. Helga's brother.'

When Bob Davison called, Daniel expected to hear news of Abel. Davison, however, appeared to know nothing. 'Not a word, Daniel. Most unlike him. I can only assume that everything's going fine. What I was wondering, though, was whether you and I could get together and set our house in order, so to speak. What about a meal or a drink?'

When he met Davison the next day, in spite of his having initiated the meeting, Daniel noticed that he was breathless and ill at ease as he opened the door, although he rallied soon enough to say, 'Daniel, my dear fellow. Come in.'

He was effusive. Abnormally so, Daniel thought. And over-dressed. Whereas in his student days Davison had been able to carry off his extravagant wardrobe with a considerable flair, the passage of time seemed to have worn away the spirit and sense of fun, making one uncomfortably aware of each piece of clothing and the underlying obesity it helped to disguise.

Looking around him, it appeared to Daniel that the flat had been very quickly shaken down, the furniture hastily rearranged, the cushions put straight, the table cleared. There was, underneath the surface order of the place, a very strong suggestion of disarray. This last quality he noticed equally in Davison himself. His clothes were creased, ruffled and out of order. There was a tension too about the man, as though Daniel's arrival had been wrongly timed and had caught him before he'd had the opportunity to compose himself.

'Sorry about this business, Dan,' Davison began, fussing

around him, mixing drinks, lighting a cigarette, and every now and again pushing a balled-up handkerchief up to his forehead and sweeping it impatiently round to his temples. 'I'd have thought by now you'd have been able to sort things out with Abel. You know, a clean slate. New beginning, and all the rest of it. Can't understand it, not being able to get hold of him.'

'I know where he is,' Daniel said. 'That's not the point any-more.' He sipped slowly at the Scotch. 'In fact, I went down to the workshop.'

Davison looked at him uneasily, with the handkerchief still crumpled in his fist. 'Yes? You didn't see him?'

'The point is that I didn't want to.'

An uneasy smile played briefly on Davison's face. 'Oh, I don't think you should give up on him so easily,' he said.

'Give up? It's not Abel that I'm worried about so much. Not what he's doing or what he feels. He's got to make up his own mind and go his own way. I understand that now. What worries me is myself. If we did meet now . . . what would happen? What would I say to him? What is there to say? That's what's been worrying me.'

Davison poured himself a second drink then cleared his throat and said, 'I suppose you've met the rest of the gang. Helga, of course. You know her. But the others . . .?'

'Edgar?'

'Yes.' Davison's eyes opened wide and lines of tension rose up in his neck as he leaned forward slightly in his chair. In his hands the glass was turned slowly, pushed ceaselessly round and round by the fingers.

Daniel wondered what Davison's involvement with Edgar was. He'd immediately detected the importance of the question, and wondered even if this wasn't the reason behind the phone-call and the invitation for drinks. Edgar. Given Arthur's interpretation of Edgar's behaviour, and given the fact that he was Helga's brother, then he could understand his interest in Jenny, and even understand the occasions of trespass at Rawley. But Davison could only be involved through Abel.

'You know Edgar?' Daniel asked.

'Yes. Both of them, since they were young children. Their

father was a friend of mine just after Cambridge and I parted company. And the mother . . . well, the less said about her the better. The father divorced her when Edgar would have been about seven or eight. And since then, nothing but trouble. Basically, and unlike the majority of us in these decadent times, Edgar is a moralist. A puritan of the spirit. Self-righteous and totally out of sympathy with all those things that make life worthwhile. A shame he wasn't born three hundred years ago; we could have sent him across to America.'

Davison stopped and said, 'I see that none of this comes as a surprise. You've obviously met Edgar.'

Daniel watched the play of lines on the other man's face. Slowly a series of suggestions began to flow upwards to the surface where they mingled uneasily, making him suddenly defensive and unsure of himself.

'What did you think?' Davison asked.

'What do you think of someone who's capable of destroying your property to settle an imaginary personal score? I don't know. You're in the trade. What words would you use? Mad? Adolescent? Insecure?'

Daniel felt his anger rising as each word was spoken. He turned away and looked at the carpets. The careful lines of the dresser against the far wall, and the china and cut glass which it contained. The statue of Siva in the corner, standing by itself, dark and multi-limbed on top of a small table. There was a coldness about Davison's objects, his possessions, which he'd never felt so intensely before, a coldness that was not simply the property of something without life but an evil, enervating energy that had the power to destroy the very gift of life.

'What did he do?' Davison asked. His eyes bulged, the whites lacerated by thin red veins. 'You say he went into your house?'

'With an axe,' Daniel replied.

'My God.' Davison breathed more quickly and it was then, quite suddenly, that the chaotic collection of images that had till now been merely irritating and incapable of real meaning broke through with force. It was as if Davison's fear, because it was undoubtedly fear that had forced him to arrange this meeting, had acted as a catalyst on the various elements of unrest which had been building up within him. Daniel felt his own energy soaring, and it was with unprecedented clarity and certainty that he saw Davison living in constant terror of Edgar. Davison, overwhelmed by the knowledge that in the end his possessions, his clothes, his miniatures, his statuettes and his paintings enjoyed an existence of which he was no necessary part, had turned elsewhere for an object to cultivate and embroider with his attention. And the object he'd chosen was Abel. Abel, the lifegiver. Then, jealous that some day he'd start drifting away, he'd encouraged him to take drugs, assuring him that someone in his position had no difficulty laying his hands on whatever he wanted. Wildly he noticed the irony of the situation. To Arthur Abel was the figure of death, firmly putting his seal on an entire way of life. To Davison Abel was life itself, a host body he could cling to until he'd sucked it dry and the time came to move on elsewhere. And in his own eyes? Daniel wavered. He didn't know.

'He was here, wasn't he?' Daniel asked.

Davison looked at him and with a quick, nervous gasp for breath said, 'Who, Edgar? Good heavens, no.'

'No. My brother. Abel.'

'Whatever makes you think that? I told you on the phone . . .'

'He was here.' Daniel's persistence momentarily surprised even himself, but as he thought back to the suggestion of disarray in the room and even in Davison himself the certainty of what had happened and had been happening perhaps for a long time became impossible to ignore.

'You bastard. No wonder he wasn't interested in staying with Helga with you and your bloody interference.'

But even as he said it and as he watched the reaction on Davison's face he knew it was not quite what had happened. 'Or did you make him?' he added, certain now that Davison had forced Abel into leaving Helga.

'Really, Daniel, this is going too far. I've always been a friend to Abel. Helped him when he needed it. Given him all the assistance I could. I don't see that I deserve to be abused for it.'

'And now you're worried about Edgar finding out,' Daniel said, ignoring the protestation. 'Both you and Jenny Hallowes. What kind of people are you?'

'No, you've got it wrong, Dan. I've never touched Abel, I swear it. My God, it wouldn't be proper. Don't you think I haven't got a sense of decency left? With others, yes. I can't deny that. But not Abel.'

He didn't even try to resist as Daniel struck out at him. He hit him only once, but it was enough to throw him to the floor. As he lifted his head from the carpet Daniel could see that his mouth was cut, and blood flowed freely on to his shirt and jacket.

'Don't,' Davison said, lifting his hand to protect his face. 'Don't do it again.'

The strength that erupted within him hardly seemed to be his own. It came out of the depths and flowed along the veins of his body so fast that he wasn't able to direct it let alone attempt any control. Within seconds he had overturned most of the furniture, picking up the ornaments, the pictures, the carefully selected and cherished bronzes and porcelain and throwing them to the floor. How long the destruction went on Daniel didn't know, but it seemed to him only a short time before he had exhausted himself, before his breath had started to catch, and he had to support himself against the wall for fear of falling to the floor.

Davison remained where he was. His face was quite white, and in horrible contrast to the blood that still flowed from his mouth. Finally, however, he gestured weakly with his hand and said, 'Please. Please don't break any more of my things.'

The reason Daniel gave himself for going to see Jenny was that he wanted to warn her that he felt Edgar was someone to be taken very seriously. It was ironic, he reflected, that whereas Edgar's intrusion into his own life had not made him think this way, the video recording in the workshop and Bob Davison's overt fear had convinced him readily enough. In spite of everything that had happened he found it impossible to dismiss Jenny. It was probable, he knew, that she had merely used him, but he couldn't eradicate the memories of the times they'd spent together nor the very real physical longing he'd had for her.

It was with a curious anticipation and sense of excitement that he set out on the Friday evening for London. In fact, it had not been an easy decision to come to. He had spent almost a week alone at Rawley, shut off from everyone else, frightened not only by what he had done to Davison but frightened by what was happening to him in general. The worst of it all was that he couldn't accurately describe what was going on, either outside the house, or within his own mind and body.

The conflict, at its most basic level, was between the sense of perspective which he had grown up with over the years, and the confusing and disordered events which he was being forced to observe. His own experience and his own particular vision told him that it was possible to fit events into an orderly pattern. The world was capable of description without resorting to magic, or mystery, or even to God. He was a child of reason, and all things about him had a just and logical cause. His faith in mankind involved a basic faith in his ability to understand whatever predicaments he might meet. He believed in a norm. He believed that generally man was a reasonable creature and that his aberrations, however horrible, however numerous, were nothing more than aberrations, and should not be considered as indicative of basic evil or any other nonsense. The universe was an ordered system, whether that system were understood or not. For every effect there was a cause, and what he needed more than anything else was the faith to survive until he learnt to understand. There was room in the world for wonder, but not for mystery; for respect, but not for fear.

During the week that followed his abortive attempt to see his brother he spent much of the time re-reading Arthur's books. There was, it was true, much to enjoy. And there was a private reward in recognising here and there a mutual friend, a face one had forgotten, or a particular conversation one had had and now was used as part of a different structure. But what struck him most, especially in the last two books, was Arthur's increasing use of symbol and esoteric reference. Men and women and their normal day-to-day lives seemed to play less and less part. Instead, there was more calling-up of so-called spiritual things, of the mystery of place, such as might be found in Powys or even Hardy. But Arthur was going much further in that he seemed to have begun to spend his time more on random musings, long flights of comment and hypothesis which used human nature as a touchstone, but which could not correctly be called anything but theorising, and then only at the cheapest of levels.

All this came to him as something of a shock because he had always been one of Arthur's main apologists. He had believed in his optimism. He had been taken in completely by his outward show of seriousness. But the more he read the more he felt that Arthur had taken refuge from the real world in a mist of sentimentality, with one exception only, and that was when he returned to the subject of violence. One paragraph in a short story struck him in particular:

'"And who is Grendel?" the narrator asked. "Simple, you tell me. Grendel is the monster killed by Beowulf. A legend. I accept that. But Grendel also has echoes which stretch back to the days of primitive man, when the forces of the unknown were given the shapes of wild beasts and giants, and strange monsters living in caves or beneath the waters of seas and lakes. There we meet a people who saw themselves not as things separate from the world in which they lived, but an integral part of it. For primitive man all objects, alive or not, formed part of a spiritual whole. Essentially he and the world were one. Seen in this context the men and women did not lead separate lives. The individual consciousness was as yet undeveloped. Instead there were groups, and a vague collective consciousness which acted as a group mind, collecting and interpreting information, and arriving finally at symbols which were to blossom into individual conceptual thought. Grendel was a product of those early days. He was a creature living in a lake, but in reality the lake was the substance of the group mind. Grendel, in fact, did not live outside the group, but inside. Grendel was part of man, and man part of Grendel . . . the long battle of mankind over these thousands of years has partly been to banish his animal vices. Evolution is the story of the battle between mind and body, and perhaps it is true to say that mind only appears to have won because it is capable of the greater deception. In fact, Grendel is alive in each one of us. You and I, we are Beowulf. But we are also Grendel, and like Grendel we prey on our rational selves. If the rational self should weaken, then Grendel takes over. The day darkens. Clouds gather over the surface of the lake. And as the light disappears a hand breaks through the thin ice that covers the water. This is the time to be afraid, because the ultimate lesson of Beowulf is that each one of us has to fight that battle." '

This was on a different level altogether because the sentimentality was well hidden beneath a seemingly powerful exterior. The symbol of Grendel was not a new one in Arthur's very personal mythology. Daniel had known of it from almost the first days of his acquaintance with him. However, it was here written down in its most developed form, and although he distrusted the basic argument – that there were two separate forces operating within each person's nature – it was nevertheless a popular one and somehow very disturbing. The myth of duality, of the inseparability of good and evil, of the flow between masculine and feminine, of the narrow line between life and death, was absolutely basic to all of Arthur's work, and it was partly because it was so strong that men like Gordon Spence, to say nothing of the more established critics, were so ready to attack him. To such men Arthur's books smacked of predeterminism, of trends and patterns that were so firmly established that human development could only take place within the constraints they laid down. For his own part, Daniel distrusted the basic argument because he had been conditioned to distrust it. He had none of his father's or the older generations of Rosses' faith in the ultimate compassion of a benevolent God; he believed instead in the eventual triumph of his own reason. He believed that the limits of personal achievement depended entirely on the patterns created by the human mind. He stood or fell on the faith he had in his capacity to struggle to overcome his own ignorance. As for Arthur's argument that all men were Jekyll and Hyde, each one capable of great good and great evil, he found it worthless in the actual evaluation of human relationships. Taken too far it led irretrievably to sentimentality. It allowed Raskolnikov to be saved by a prostitute. It allowed Macbeth to deliver some of the greatest lines in the history of the English language. It allowed Hitler to be idolised by the Nazis. But for all this to happen the facts had to be forgotten. Raskolnikov murdered an old woman. Macbeth murdered his king. And Grendel? Grendel was nothing more than a fable, a tale of a monster living at the bottom of a lake, who from time to time would come out of his lair and lay waste the villages and the people of the surrounding countryside. That was all. There was nothing more.

As he drove into town that evening Daniel's main preoccupation was what he would say to Jenny. He was worried too by what she would say to him, or if indeed there was any ground left for communication at all. In some ways Jenny was a test case, as in his confusion he felt that if he could set things straight with her then he would be on the right path to sorting out the chaos that existed elsewhere. His concern for Jenny was also a means of distracting himself from his impending divorce. Within a few weeks the divorce was expected to be through, and he had no doubt at all that Ponting wouldn't want to waste any time worrying about the niceties of the situation. Julie married to Ponting. It was not something he could think about for long without registering both anger and frustration. As far as Jenny's relationship with Helga was concerned he had not allowed himself to accept it as anything more than a purely fleeting encounter. The image of the two of them together was so grotesque that he found it impossible to seriously consider. And yet he could not dismiss the purposefulness with which Jenny had tracked Helga down, nor the very singleminded way in which for the past few years she had maintained such a careful balance between her relationship with Arthur and himself on the one hand, and with Helga on the other. Scheming, yes, he could allow that. But he did not wish to think that Lillian Feather's verdict – that Jenny Hallowes lived in an isolated world, exclusive, selfish, and which she ruled like a queen – was right, either.

Without questioning what he was doing he stopped every now and again and had a few drinks. He drove the car slowly down the embankment from Vauxhall to Putney. When he crossed the river he registered that he had gone much farther to the east than was necessary, but the fact made little impression. He stopped in Chelsea and again in Fulham. As the evening wore on he imagined conversations between Jenny and himself. He rehearsed lines, and even produced a prologue, a middle and an end – an ending which in fact was a happier conclusion to that abortive attempt to spend the night with her in the hotel. He lingered over the idea. Bitterly he reflected that he had allowed himself to be used. But after a time he started to wonder if maybe Lillian hadn't gone too far and exaggerated the relationship between Jenny and Helga. It was, after all, a ludicrous conjunction. Helga, the spoilt middle-class brat, and Jenny, the abused and perhaps even masochistic intellectual. No. If her own sex were what Jenny craved, then it would have been far more her style to have rooted among the burrows of Bethnal Green or Brixton for her accomplices. Helga might have appealed to Jenny on another level, for without doubt there was something totally amoral about the girl. It was possible that in her Jenny had seen an abstraction of her own self – the side of herself her own intelligence had not allowed to take over. The hopeless, damned side of Helga. The child offering her body to an indifferent society.

But when he thought of Edgar his thoughts cleared and he knew for certain that Jenny was in danger. And had been too, probably, for a long time. Edgar, guarding his sister like some medieval knight set against the primeval forests. Edgar, the tormented product of a world where men and women attempted contact with words and ideas that had long since been raped and pillaged beyond repair.

He arrived at the front door slightly tense but in a good enough humour. He knocked loudly at first, then when no one came to the door shouted out his name.

The door opened a few inches.

'Jenny?'

'She's not in.'

Daniel swayed on the doorstep. 'Seem to have got the wrong house,' he said, momentarily confused.

The door then opened to about forty-five degrees and he found himself staring at what appeared to be a young girl. Her hair was wet and there was water on her face. He stared at the bathrobe and the thought crossed his mind that underneath she was wearing nothing.

'Helga, I didn't recognise you.'

She watched him nervously and slowly began to close the door.

Daniel pushed his hand against the closing door and said, 'Come on now, you wouldn't lock out an old friend, would you?' Once inside the house he took off his coat and said, 'Don't tell me you didn't recognise me.'

She stood up against the wall of the hallway, her eyes wide, watching him.

'Where's Jenny?' he asked.

'She went out.'

He followed her into the living-room, and it was only then that it occurred to him that Helga very likely had no idea at all of his own relationship with Jenny. She followed him into the living-room, clutching the bathrobe round her, although it was well tied at the waist. Her feet, he noticed, left damp marks on the carpet.

For a time his attention strayed from her. He stared around at the familiar room, except that here and there he recognised the intrusion of another personality. Photographs. Odd pieces of pottery. A large teddy bear standing in the corner.

'Must be a bit of a shock, my barging in like this,' he said.

She had sat down in an armchair, though she kept close to the front of it as though ready to leap up at a moment's notice.

'How did you find me?' she asked.

It was some time before he was able to interpret the question properly, but when he did it was clear that Helga saw his visit in relation to herself, rather than in relation to Jenny. He hedged a little before saying, 'Someone told me.'

'Who? No one knows. No one.'

He was brought up by that. 'You're obviously wrong. I knew, for a start.'

'Who was it?' She was so nervous that her hands moved perpetually across the front of her body and her feet scuffed and pulled across the carpet.

'Jenny,' he said without thinking.

She stared at him for some time before shaking her head. 'It wasn't her. It couldn't have been.'

'You seem very certain.'

She shook her head violently, then calmed down and stared at him. There was a disconcerting conflict between the calmness in her face and the urgent tension in her body. Daniel looked at her and, through the numbness of the drink and the general confusion of his own senses, saw the body of a woman, with the movement and fullness of a woman's body.

'You'll find that Jenny's not so straightforward as you might think,' he said. 'But perhaps you already know that.'

She looked away towards the door as though she had heard a movement in the corridor outside. When she turned back her face had broken. Her eyes moved quickly. 'Please go,' she said.

'But I've only just come. Besides, I want to talk to Jenny.'

Slowly she reached out for a cigarette. Her hands were

steadier now, and he felt relief at the action. Quite suddenly he was excited by the situation, strained and bizarre though it was. It was a game. He felt that he was enjoying himself as much as he'd done in months.

'Please go,' she repeated.

'Why?'

'Because I don't want you here.'

'Why, because you don't want me prying into your sordid little affair with Jenny Hallowes? Well, if that's the case rest assured. Uncle Daniel is just the same liberal old fool that he always was. I don't give a damn what you get up to. Why should I? You wouldn't listen. Abel wouldn't listen so why in the hell should you? Feel free. Do as you like.'

'Free?' she shot back at him. 'What makes you think I've ever been free to do what I like?'

He remembered Lillian telling him about the child. How Jenny had forced her to walk out on it. Daniel had a brief vision of his grandfather intoning passages out of the Bible. Judgement of the wicked. The dead child paying for the sins of its parents.

'I'm sorry,' he said. The apology was directionless. It fell uneasily from him. 'How about a drink?' he said more cheerfully, and then went across to the sideboard.

'You know your way around very well,' she said as he fixed himself a Scotch.

'Oh yes. Sort of a family friend. Have one yourself?'

She watched as he poured a small measure into her glass. Just as he was about to replace the cap on the bottle he watched himself add a little more. It happened so fast that he was unable to question or control the action.

Helga drank it absent-mindedly. Then, looking up from her glass, she said, 'Will you go now?' It was an appeal. There was even a certain petulance in her voice.

'No, I think I'll stay. Jenny and I have something to talk about.'

'She won't be back.'

'You mean she's gone out of town?' He thought of Arthur. It seemed impossible that she could so cold-bloodedly arrange the hours and days of her life.

Helga nodded. 'Tomorrow. She said she'd be back then. Now please have your drink and go. I'll tell her you were here.'

Daniel eyed his glass. 'What about another one? Yours too.' He reached for her glass.

She stood up suddenly. 'Why are you doing this? You've got no right.'

He could see then what Jenny saw in her. It was not simply Helga, the flesh-and-blood human being. But Helga the idea, the desecrated image.

'I'm not feeling too well. In fact, I was just going to bed when you came. I was having . . .'

But why had Abel left her? Because he had had enough of her, had taken what he wanted and then decided that the time had come to go? No, that was ridiculous. Abel was incapable of such cynicism. For a moment he had an image which was quite different to his interpretation of Helga a few seconds earlier. Abel and Helga together, attempting to survive in a world which they'd had no part in building.

'I was having a bath,' she repeated.

Actually in love with each other, and the child a product of that love. But the child was dead.

'If Abel loved you then why did he leave?' he asked, turning on her suddenly.

She stared at him, shattered by the change he'd taken.

'And how could you leave the child?' he asked.

She thought for a while before saying, 'Have you seen Abel?' The stress she gave the words implied that his question was redundant. He knew then that she was telling him that Abel was incapable of staying with her. Why? He struggled silently for an answer, and saw only pictures of Bob Davison lying on the floor with his hand raised to guard his face. Davison, the parasite. And Abel, already exhausted, incapable.

'How did Davison ever get away with it?' he asked, but so quietly it was as though he'd asked himself.

She laughed, and he knew instinctively that it was a challenge. If Edgar held him to blame then perhaps she did too.

'Abel was incapable of even lifting a finger for himself,' she said. She sat down again and played with her glass. Without thinking Daniel took it from her and refilled it. 'And what I was expected to do with a man like that I don't know.' She stared at him resentfully. 'You think it's so easy. You add things up. All the items you can think of. And then you come to your conclusions. Well, that's all very well if you and I are adding up the same things. But we're not. You don't know what in the hell is happening. What was Abel to you? And what do you want him to be for me? Why don't you open your eyes and see what's going on out there? You have to survive. You have to.' She reached for another cigarette. Daniel stared helplessly at her face, finding it confusingly old and worn, swept as it was now by tracks of dirt and makeup that coursed down her cheeks with the tears.

'Why didn't you come to me for help?' he asked.

She smiled. 'What kind of help?'

He shrugged his shoulders, lost for words, then let his eyes wander down the front of her bathrobe.

'I don't want to be here,' she said next, surprising him by the dejection in her voice. 'I swore I'd never come back. I lay awake at night praying that she wouldn't come, that she wouldn't make me. But she did come, and I couldn't say no.' She laughed, but the laughter was forced, and for a moment or two he himself was aware of the chaos of emotions it masked. 'That's always been my trouble. I could never stand up for myself, never say no.' She looked into her glass. 'I always thought I was going to be hurt, and I couldn't stand that. Pain. Any kind of pain. I'd do anything not to be hurt.'

The confession baffled him. Drops of water still ran down her legs, and he stared at the damp patches on the carpet near her feet. She shivered.

'If only you'd all leave us alone.'

He felt her slowly excising him, removing him to a safe distance. The plea was meant to wound, and wounded he cut back, and said, 'But Edgar won't. You're quite prepared to have him run around acting out some vigilante's dream-world.'

'No. No.' She shook her head. 'You think any of us can stop Edgar? You think we haven't tried? But he's always been this way, ever since he was a young boy. Always the same.' She looked through him, her glass held limply in one hand.

'You said he was harmless,' Daniel said, conscious now of a rising anger. 'That time when I went to see you in the hospital. "Oh, don't worry about Edgar," you said. "He's just curious, that's all." As though I were some kind of zoo that he could contemplate and examine at his own free will. The truth is that your brother's sick, Helga. He's sick and he should bloody well be in a State hospital. The last thing he needs is the likes of Lillian Feather and her travelling circus performing good works and delivering homilies on the delinquency of modern youth. Edgar's a maniac, but all I see is people either trying to shut him out of their minds, pretending he doesn't exist, or like me, yes me too, pretending that it's something that doesn't really matter. But not now, I can tell you that. He scares me, but unlike Jenny and Bob Davison I intend to do something about it.'

No sooner had he finished than he realised just how improbable it would be for him to do anything. In time Helga would laugh at him. As they all had done.

'I don't know how to stop him,' he heard her say.

He remembered the video monitor and that familiar but terrifying ride through the streets of Putney, until the camera had stopped outside Jenny's front door.

'Thank God he doesn't know,' she said.

He looked up at her. The camera had caught Helga coming to the door of the house, the very house in which he now sat talking to her. She thought her brother knew nothing of the affair with Jenny Hallowes. But she was wrong.

'What makes you think he doesn't?'

'No. It's impossible. He mustn't know.'

He resisted the impulse to tell her, and found that by doing so he had gained an advantage over her which was so strong in nature that it temporarily erased everything else that had come before.

'You're trying to make me drunk,' she said, as he filled her glass again.

Polly Adams had called her a slut. Lillian too had implied as much. The spoiled daughter of a spoiled mother, dragged up through the mire of a middle-class existence where sex was easy currency. The way she sat there now, her legs apart pushing the bathrobe taut across her knees, and her hair wet and clinging to her neck.

'I've a damn good mind to tell him,' Daniel said.

She threw her head back and stared at him, eyes wide open. 'No. Please God don't do that.'

He laughed and went across to her.

There were times when he was to remember apologising to her, going to the door, opening it, and finding himself a little later in his car. There were other times when he remembered their laughing together, drinking the entire bottle of Scotch between them, and then his waking up at about three in the morning to find Helga vomiting on the carpet at the foot of the bed. But in clearer moments he knew that he had forced her away from the living-room and into the bedroom. If he concentrated long enough he could bring back other memories. He remembered her on the floor at his feet. He remembered ripping the bathrobe from her and throwing it across the bottom of the bed. And he would recall waking to find her sobbing and kneeling in her own vomit. When he had dressed it had been in silence, a silence which was only broken when she followed him to the bedroom door and said, 'I never asked you to come here. For God's sake, please go.'

For three days Daniel hid himself in an hotel room, eating infrequently, indifferent to his personal appearance. His concern was not so much with the reasons for what had happened, but with the act itself. What he wanted above all else was a means of purging himself from what he had done; an actual understanding of it all he knew would not have helped in the slightest. He was plagued, nevertheless, by the suggestion that Helga had led him on, that she had seduced him, a suggestion which constantly foundered on his own personal shame and the need to eliminate the entire incident from his mind. He was prepared to do anything that was necessary in order to recreate what he had destroyed.

Yet the more he put his mind to it the less capable he was of imagining what he might do in order to reconstruct what had been there before, and the more certain he was that his treatment of Helga was only a single element in a vast pattern of change over which he had almost no control. The truth was that he had, knowingly or not, contributed to the collapse of those values which had so far supported him, and it was no more than a wish born of despair and perhaps fear as well that made him want to recreate things as they were. Destruction, he discovered, was permanent, and the effort to rebuild the past almost certainly worthless.

At the end of the third day he had convinced himself that he could do nothing except return to Rawley and live with himself, a decision he came to with difficulty as with the passing of time the thought of going back on to the streets seemed less and less inviting.

It was about six o'clock. The light, the noise of the traffic, the colour and size of the buildings, all seemed to arouse different responses than they had done in the past. He was distanced from these surroundings and completely without the comfort he had at Rawley of feeling at home in his environment. He did not belong. The activity of the people, the cars on the road, even the noise of his feet on the pavement were all part of a world which did not quite coincide with the one with which he was familiar.

He did not wander aimlessly. Before driving back to Rawley he had decided to go down to the Embankment and walk along to Whitehall, perhaps even getting as far as Charing Cross and the Strand. He told himself that this would do him good, that the sight of familiar buildings and the actual physical exertion would help to reunite the disparate and disorganised forces within his body.

With this in mind he set out at a good pace and had not gone too far when he saw, not more than seventy-five yards ahead of him, a motorcyclist pulled up at the side of the road. He was sitting astride his machine, but even at this distance it was possible to hear the engine running.

Daniel stopped and stared in front of him. Fair hair. Blue denim jacket. The back slightly hunched forward. He remembered the bike parked at the gate at Rawley. And Edgar walking across the lawn. Unable to move he was struck by the certainty that the motorbike was not there by accident. It was there for him.

He looked quickly up and down the road and was immediately reassured by the number of people going in either direction. He was perfectly safe. Nothing could happen. A few moments later, when the engine was revved loudly and the motorcyclist pulled out into the traffic, he even managed to laugh out loud. With one or two heads turned his way he set out across the road at a diagonal, having come to the decision that instead of taking the walk he had intended he would return to the car and drive straight back to Rawley. It was when he was about halfway across that he realised that the machine had been turned round and was in fact very close to him. The quick reversal of direction caused him to panic. He ran forward a few steps, then stopped. As he did so he heard the screech of brakes, and then immediately afterwards the heavy gunning of the engine. He moved forward again, running quickly towards the kerb. It was on this last lap that they collided.

Daniel was never really sure what happened exactly, but he did recall later that they both ended up in the road, the rider a few yards to one side of his bike, and Daniel himself just by the kerb. They were neither badly hurt. For his own part he had a bruised shoulder and thigh, and his suit was torn. He paid little attention to the condition of the rider, though he did recall the look of anger, and the shouting, though not the words, which were lost in the sound of the traffic.

Had this happened under different circumstances then he would have undoubtedly gone to the police. As it was his one reaction was to get away. The incident had scared him badly, and all he longed for was the presence of surroundings with which he was familiar. He wanted Rawley, the comfort of Rawley, the security that it offered.

He drove home quickly and without futher incident, though he arrived somewhat stiff and still shocked by what had happened. The day, however, was not to end easily. Polly met him on the front porch. As soon as she saw him get out of the car she rushed across and said, 'Did they tell you, Mr Daniel? Did they tell you about it?'

He stared at her without comprehension. It was only after some time that he realised she was herself so shaken and excited that she could not even see his own condition.

'The fire,' she said.

'What fire?'

'The stables.' Needlessly, she raised her arm and pointed.

Even so he would not have learnt very much if Walter Perkins had not been there. He came out of the house and immediately commented on what Polly had so far failed to notice.

'An accident,' Daniel said. 'Nothing at all. My fault altogether.'

Perkins stared at him then turned and pointed to the house. 'You're lucky. Could have been a pile of cinders by now.'

'What happened?'

'Wiring. That's what they said.'

He got the story slowly as Perkins took his time over tea and a plateful of toast. On purpose, Daniel thought. His gestures, the length of the words, all done for effect. He couldn't help suspecting that he was delighting in every second of it. The fire had broken out about ten o'clock two nights earlier. Polly had phoned him to say that there'd been a sudden explosion out at the back of the house and all the lights had gone out. Like the war, Polly had put it. Perkins had then told her to get outside on the lawn and wait till he came over. Meanwhile he'd phoned the fire brigade, who arrived to find a small-scale fire raging in the stables. Calmly Perkins said that it wasn't much, but added that with the general condition of the wiring in the house perhaps it wasn't too surprising.

'Ought to consider yourself lucky,' he said. 'Could have been the whole place.'

Later on Daniel went with them and had a look at the damage. It was dark by this time, a little after ten o'clock. He carried a torch with him and cast the beam around among the blackened timbers and the muddy area outside long enough for Perkins to ask him what he was looking for.

He found them at last. Tyre marks outside the stable entrance. Single tracks, ending in a skid mark in the mud.

'You didn't hear anything that night?' he asked Polly. 'Engine noise? Someone revving an engine?'

'Nothing,' she said firmly. Her eyes held his and he turned away, throwing the beam of the torch once more across the tracks on the ground.

Daniel first heard about Jenny's accident two days after returning to Rawley. He had just settled into the morning paper when the phone rang.

'Daniel? This is Norma.'

She was breathless, excited.

'Norma, if it's about Friday . . .'

But she obviously had no time for discussion of their weekly dinners. 'Daniel, what in God's name have you been up to? Bob Davison has been round here and appears to think that you've gone out of your mind. Said that in his opinion you were unbalanced. That sort of thing.'

He managed a short, strangled laugh before saying, 'Bob managed to say that? And what else did he tell you? That I'd been trying to get into his bed?'

'Don't be ridiculous, Dan. Unless, of course, Bob has been telling me a pack of lies. Which I have no reason to believe. You have, you must admit, been under a great deal of strain, darling.'

'If you want to use medical jargon, then yes. Yes, I've been under more bloody strain than I want to think about, but that doesn't give Davison any right to go laying down the moral code. What did he tell you?'

'That you came in, drunk, he believed, and started yelling at him for trying to put your brother back on to the straight and narrow. You know how I feel about Abel, Daniel. I had to agree with Bob; something had to be done. Somebody had to do something and I don't know whether it was because of Julie or what it was but you just didn't seem capable. I'm sure Bob's done a marvellous job with Abel.'

'Oh, you can say that again.'

'Now just what is that meant to mean?'

Daniel contemplated the phone in his hand, then heard Norma's voice once again babbling at the other end. When he listened in he heard, 'What made you do it?'

'What did he say I did?'

'Lay into him with a stick.'

'With a stick! For Christ's sake, Norma. Can you see me walking past Kensington Gardens and into Lancaster Gate with a stick so that I could bash Bob Davison?'

'But you did strike him, nevertheless. Whatever it was. He's got a bruised lip and broken teeth to show for it.'

'Good.' Daniel swallowed hard and ignored Norma's confusion at the other end.

'Now, what I'm suggesting is that I arrange to get the two of you together,' she said later. 'We'll have a crowd over, so it won't be too obvious or embarrassing for you. I really don't see any reason why in this day and age two grown men should resort to such silly adolescent antics. And especially as we're such old friends. I always thought Bob was such a character. What do you say?'

He remained silent in face of the onslaught. Norma was a rock. Nothing could move her.

'Anything else, Norma? I seem to have a lot of things to catch up with all of a sudden. Work.' He gestured with his hand towards an imaginary backlog of things undone in the house around him.

'Yes,' she said. 'Yes, there is. Arthur's wife had an accident.'

He froze, his hand clutched tightly round the phone.

'You know Jenny, Daniel? I mean you know her quite well, don't you?'

'What happened?'

'Nobody's quite sure. Late at night and she was very drunk, weaving about the road, probably, because there was no reason for her to be out walking so late at night in Putney. I mean Putney, of all places. Someone, one of the neighbours, heard a motorbike, and then a woman screaming. But they didn't actually see anything. The bastard made off, of course. Typical late-night hit and run.'

He hesitated before asking, 'How is she?'

'She's in a coma. Skull fracture. God knows what else. I keep thinking of poor Arthur . . .'

Daniel let the phone drop into the cradle. As he made his way back into the living-room he noticed that Polly was standing at the bottom of the stairs, watching him.

Afraid to contact Arthur and determined to shut all thoughts of Edgar out of his mind, Daniel remained isolated at Rawley. Summer had settled in and with it a spell of languidness that he plunged into eagerly, evoking memories from the earliest days of his childhood in an attempt to avoid the threat of dwelling on what had happened between Edgar and Jenny. Walking down the old coach track at the bottom of the lawn, or around the kitchen garden, he would find himself arrested by the memory of a cricket ball on wood, of voices heard at a great distance, of himself looking at the house from the far end of the drive and being totally overwhelmed by its size. The heat piled up with the days, and the nights were no longer any relief. Polly wilted, and in the end begged permission to take herself off for a few days to a friend who ran a boarding house in Eastbourne. With Polly gone, apart from the odd-job gardener who came in for a few hours each day from the village, he was left totally to himself.

Yet it had always been true of Rawley that one could never be completely alone. Actual physical isolation was an illusion that could never be enjoyed for very long before the past crept up and peopled the corners and shadows of the house with creatures and spirits that had lived and died years before one had even been born. It was not necessary to believe in ghosts to accept that Rawley was capable of creating its own lifeforms. Within Rawley the past had never really died; it might, perhaps, be occasionally forgotten, but there could be no real death while the wood and the stone, the pictures and the cloth, the furniture and the air itself all spoke so certainly of the years that had gone. His father and mother. His grandfather. George Hutchinson. And all the Rosses, right back to Edward Ross, whose unpublished papers on

Indian flora and fauna lay neatly packaged in a box upstairs. Even when looking out of the window at the land around Rawley it was impossible for one's vision not to be tainted by the place where one was standing. Rawley had a grip on all those who lived within it, a grip that struck to the very depths of the imaginative spirit and of the emotions. All this Daniel now knew to be true. He had become a slave to Rawley, a slave to his own memories of what it had given him and meant to him in the past, a slave to its constant demands on his physical presence. For the first time during these days he saw Rawley as a vast parasite, a succubus that had mated with his imagination and in so doing nearly sucked it dry. And the heat only made it worse. He felt listless. Trapped. Devoid of energy.

Arthur arrived unexpectedly on the Saturday morning, and having searched the house unsuccessfully for some time found Daniel reading in one corner of the kitchen garden. Daniel saw him as he walked on the far side of the wall, his unmistakable gait evident in the movement of his head as it bobbed up and down above the old stonework.

'Empty,' Arthur said, indicating the house.

'Polly's off. Eastbourne.'

Arthur pulled out an old deck-chair that lay up against the wall. As he moved it out a lizard ran swiftly up the wall before disappearing finally behind some moss.

'She wants to die in Eastbourne,' Daniel said. After a time he added, 'And Abel wanted to die in Mexico.' He fell silent, thinking of Jenny lying unconscious in her hospital room.

'You heard?' Arthur asked.

'Yes.' Daniel looked at him from behind the safety of his sunglasses. He'd known all along that Arthur would come, but now that he had he was pleasantly surprised at how unflustered he felt. 'I'm sorry,' he said. He noticed that Arthur looked worn, the face cracked and unexpectedly old.

Arthur blinked in the sunlight, and when he spoke his voice was quiet and withdrawn as though it too were overwhelmed by the unusual intensity of the day. 'I always knew, of course,' he said. 'You and Jenny. And Helga. But I didn't want to lose her. I would have agreed to anything.'

The admission took Daniel completely by surprise, not so

much because he hadn't been aware of Arthur's knowledge, but because he was overcome by the unexpected depth of feeling.

'I had to keep her, at whatever price. I didn't mind. And for Jenny it couldn't really have been any other way.' He looked intently at Daniel, as if trying to physically project his feelings across the gap between them. 'You see, she was too frightened of people to have the courage to give everything to one person.' Daniel listened, horrified by the simpleness of Arthur's explanation. 'That's why she tried to share it out. A little here. A little there. That way she thought she'd be safe.' He smiled. 'Ironical, isn't it?'

'Was it an accident?' Daniel asked.

'You know the answer to that. But as for proof? I have no proof.'

'You could try to find him,' Daniel suggested.

'No. Edgar's disappeared. Nobody knows where he is. And even if I did find him, what then? What would I do?' He shut his eyes briefly.

'Perhaps he didn't do it,' Daniel said. 'She was drunk. You know that.'

'Yes, I know that. Helga left her. There was a note lying on the table saying that she was leaving.'

Daniel stared straight in front of him, admitting nothing. A little later he turned to Arthur and said, 'What does Edgar want? You say there doesn't have to be a reason, but that's too easy. He has to want something.'

'I don't know.' Arthur lit a cigarette and then, preoccupied by his wife, said, 'Jenny would do things I couldn't understand. Crazy things. At times it was almost as though she enjoyed the act of destruction.'

Arthur would never understand or let himself even contemplate her selfishness, Daniel thought. There would always be excuses. Always a way to justify what she had done. Until she had made the mistake of forcing Helga to leave the baby, and he'd been unable to ignore it in her any more. Confused, bitterly hurt – Daniel felt that he could understand the violence that had taken hold of him. And thinking about what Arthur had just said about Jenny, he recalled the almost triumphant way in which she had shown her body to him that day in Putney. It occurred to Daniel then that what Arthur hadn't realised was that Jenny's chief object of destruction had not been anything outside of her. She had wanted to destroy herself. Arthur's image of an insecure woman carefully arranging her life for the benefit of her own protection was nothing but another of his sentimental interpretations of fact. Jenny had known about Edgar for a long time, aware of what he was capable and the kind of danger she was letting herself in for. Why, then, had she not left Helga alone? It was almost as though she had deliberately set out to court Edgar, willing him on, taunting him until he could stand it no more.

'She won't live, Daniel. They say she hasn't got a chance.'

Daniel watched Arthur's face, noticing the tension around the mouth. 'If there's anything I can do to help . . .'

Arthur looked at him belligerently, the eyes for a moment suddenly intense with enormous anger.

'I'm offering you my sympathy, damn it,' Daniel said.

Arthur stood up and started to walk away. Daniel called out to him but Arthur continued round to the front of the house without once looking back. Daniel followed him for a few minutes, his eyes set on the broad expanse of back and the head bent slightly forwards, before Arthur left the property and took the path across the fields towards the village.

Later on in the afternoon he was joined unexpectedly by Norma and Gordon Spence. However, when Julie arrived some five minutes afterwards he was sure that the gathering had been planned ahead of time, and specifically for his benefit.

As it was he was happy enough to be pushed around, and when he found himself driving them all up to Regent's Park he was perfectly at ease and prepared to enjoy himself.

Finding himself alone with Julie once inside the zoo he said, 'Are you going to tell me why?'

'Why what?'

'This sudden concern for my well-being. Which is what it all seems to be about. Or are you merely trying to lay ghosts before your wedding?'

'No, of course not. But I did want to see you. Afterwards it might not be so sensible.'

He smiled at her choice of words. 'But I see that dear old Charles didn't share your ambition.'

'You never change, do you?'

They walked up to the bear pit and looked in. 'You're quite wrong there. You'd be surprised at how much I've changed.'

'I know it sounds trite, but I'll miss you, Daniel. I'll miss your sense of humour.'

'But I'm being quite serious,' he said, putting his arm around her shoulders.

'Charles is a little dry sometimes. But he is dependable. And he has ambition. I need that, Dan.' She sounded apologetic.

'And he controls himself admirably,' he added. 'He's not a rapist. Unlike me.'

She laughed. 'Don't be ridiculous.'

'I'm not.' He showed her his teeth. 'I rape young girls.' He looked away from her, and then, irate at the purposeless meanderings of the bears, said, 'Why in the hell did we have to come here?'

She turned away and started walking round to the other side of the pit. 'What happened between you and Bob?' she asked, once he'd caught up with her.

'So, that's what it's all about,' he said. 'Sort of friendly inspection of the local maniac, is it?'

'What did happen, Dan? Bob said you suddenly went wild. For no reason at all.'

'He said that?' He looked at her and remembered her as she'd been as a child. Sudden panic swept through him, wave after wave of nausea gripping his stomach and making him want to reach out to her for support. In an hour or so they would leave him and he'd be forced to return to Rawley alone. But he was terrified of Rawley, terrified of the weight of it, terrified that it had betrayed him before and that it would do so again.

Julie noticed the distance in his face and said, 'Daniel, are you all right?'

His hand went out to her face. She caught it, and held it there. 'What did you do?'

'I hit him.'

'Why?'

'Because . . .' and then the words stopped in his throat as he recalled Helga at the foot of the bed and then Davison lying on the floor with his hand up to his face.

'Daniel?'

'I'll miss you, Julie.' Then characteristically he blurted out, 'Do you have to marry that lout? He's got nothing that I can't give you. Nothing. I never did like him, ever since he first started slobbering around Rawley, eyeing you from a distance to see if you'd lift your dress enough to show him your knickers. Jesus, what a bloody disaster.'

'Don't talk that way, Daniel. It makes you look a fool when you aren't.'

He watched Norma and Gordon pass by on the far side. Gordon looked old, bent at the shoulders, dispirited, as though he'd somehow managed to sidle out of a cage in one of the corners of the zoo after years of captivity. Norma was holding forth. Gesticulating with one hand, while her umbrella swung freely in the other. Seeing them as they passed by she raised the umbrella in greeting.

'You always knew how to get me, didn't you?' he said to her. 'Why did you stay with me for so long?'

She shook her head, avoiding an answer.

'Inertia?'

'No, there was much more than that. There always is, isn't there? But there wasn't enough, and let's not pretend that there was.'

'What did Bob tell you, Julie?'

'He wanted me to talk to you. He's concerned about you.'

'Only because I damn nearly broke his jaw.'

She surprised him then by facing him and putting her arms round his neck. 'Don't hurt yourself, Dan. For God's sake.'

They stood there for a long time, with his face buried deep in her hair. The zoo, the people, the animals in their cages, all seemed frozen still. Even the light wind appeared to have stopped blowing.

When Daniel returned to Rawley it was to discover that Abel had been there during his absence. A piece of paper lying on the floor just inside the door bore the simple message: I'll come back later. Abel.

By this time it was eight o'clock. He had already eaten in town with the Spences, and after dropping them off on his way back had decided to have an early night. He smiled grimly as he realised that this was now out of the question. However, he was not nearly as excited by the message as he might once have been. For Abel to come down to Rawley almost certainly meant that he was in trouble, or needed help, but Daniel was uncertain that he was any longer capable of giving help. He sat down and poured himself a drink. The time for helping others had passed; it was himself that he had to look out for. Besides, he doubted that he would know what to say. His confidence was broken, and the old attitudes he no longer trusted. He attempted to imagine himself and Abel sitting in this room, each of them sunk into the heavy square armchairs, confronting one another. There was something, not absurd, but frightening in the prospect. Perhaps Helga had told him what had happened. Perhaps Davison had persuaded him, as he had persuaded Julie and the Spences, to go down and see him. Had he been wrong about Davison? They all appeared to think so.

He stood at the window and looked out across the lawn to the field beyond. It was still light. Mid-summer. His eyes narrowed and his jaw worked ceaselessly. Even he himself was aware of the tension building up in his body. No, he had not been wrong about Davison, he was sure of that. But he didn't want to see Abel. He didn't want to see any of them. Edgar, Helga, his brother. Even Arthur and the Spences. He was tired of it all, the lies and the deceit, the fabrications so laboriously set up to disguise the loneliness and fear of those who had built them. Arthur with his books, and his carefully planned existence, desperately trying to keep himself in step with his wife's machinations. The Spences, living off their bickering and dissatisfaction with each other, like carrion existing on their own offal. Even Walter Perkins, whose rise into the middle classes had ended in such rapid petrifaction, standing like a dumb sentinel on the parapets of his kingdom, waiting in vain for a daughter who despised him.

He waited impatiently over the next two hours, frequently refilling his glass and then going back to the window. Ironic, he thought, that after so much time and so much effort on his own part Abel should come to Rawley, only to find the house empty. As the time passed Daniel began to hope that his brother had changed his mind. It would make it all far easier if at this stage he were not to come. The time had come for a new start; Julie was right. Her instincts had led her away and whatever he might think of Ponting he could no longer deny that she had made the right decision in leaving Rawley. His preoccupations, with Jenny and Edgar, with his brother and Helga, were all functions of the patterns he'd set up and which now controlled him.

Move, he told himself, that was what he would do. He went back to the drinks cupboard and poured the rest of the whisky into his glass. Get away from Rawley. Leave it. The house haunted him, held him down, and instead of trying to shrug it off he'd co-operated in his own slavery by building up myth and legend in an attempt at justification.

Going into the hallway he stumbled across to the stairs. The same stairway which his mother, usually so sickly and careful of her health, had come down that morning with such abundance of energy, her face alive with such unusual excitement. He stood at the bottom and looked upwards, half certain that he'd see her again, that he'd watch her come down towards him, and then fly past towards the perplexed figure of George Hutchinson. He laughed then at the memory of George Hutchinson, spread out in the chair opposite his father. Talking heatedly about General Dyer or Napier in Sindh, Elphinstone and Curzon, the laying of the railways across the subcontinent, Simla and Darjeeling, talking with such earnestness that it seemed impossible that these events and these people were all placed at a distance of five thousand miles and one hundred years. Maniacs, the pair of them. He raised his glass in mock salute to the dead. And all the time Perkins had been building Parklands on the old lands of Rawley, building a future which they had chosen to ignore, preferring instead to cast their minds back to a past that was long dead, and treating the present with the same indifference with which Nelson had raised the eyeglass to his blind eye.

Upstairs, he opened the door to the bedroom in which he had spent so much of his time as a child. Boxes and chests lay neatly stacked against the walls and about the floor, filled with relics of the past; apart from the absence of the actual bodies there was now and always had been no small resemblance to a mausoleum. Standing in the doorway Daniel nodded in recognition of these familiar things. His grandfather's chest, brought back from the Transvaal after the Boer War. His father's tin trunk, filled with children's christening robes and a collection of carefully wrapped suits and dress shirts. The boxes in the corner, which contained the notes written by Edward Ross of his journey into Assam. Photographs on the walls, browned and stained by years of heat and humidity, of women in long dresses on the Mall at Simla. The Red Fort. Agra. The caves at Elephanta.

All false. Junk. The entire house was nothing but a refuse tip, with himself as its janitor.

The truth was that he'd never wanted Rawley. He'd envied Abel his initiative in getting out. Rawley had always held him back, lulling him with its false sense of security into an imagined and wholly unworkable idea of his position in the world.

The glass dropped from his hand and shattered on the floor. Underneath his feet the already broken pieces were ground and scattered as he made his way uneasily farther into the room. The pictures of women on the walls. Arrogant. Standing so correctly, or sitting like Queen Victoria over a vast brood of sailor-suited children. His hands swept up quickly and cleared three of the smaller pictures from the wall. Behind them the paintwork stood out stark and square in the surrounding dust and dirt. Edward Ross's boxes he pushed away from the wall and upturned on to the floor. Mounted butterflies. Drawings of elephants and peacocks. Tigers and leopards. A ceremonial sword. A drawing of Sybil, his sister. He stared hard at her, then saw her with that long Victorian dress pulled apart and her body bared for those brief few minutes before the sepoys had cut her open. Angrily he pulled at the drawers of butterflies, throwing them to one side so that the glass covers broke and the pinned insects tumbled out dry, and slowly fell apart. The destruction incensed him and he increased his aimless attack.

It was some ten minutes later, when the room was totally overturned, when he had stopped and was standing by the window, his sleeves hanging loose, his shirt open down the front, that the lights failed.

The silence that followed was complete except for the slight rattle of the panes of glass in the windows, and every now and again a trembling in the roof.

His mind cleared as his eyes adjusted to the darkness and he began to see the outlines of objects in the room. Lifting his feet slowly one after the other he made his way back to the door, cursing softly and aware of a burning pain across one wrist where he'd cut himself on broken glass.

The fuses, he told himself. But it was unlikely that they would all have gone at the same time. The wiring, then. He remembered what Perkins had said the other day when he'd come in and found that the stables had been hit by fire. He stopped, standing quite rigid. Fire. Turning his head slowly round he breathed in deeply, again and then again. There was, without doubt, the unmistakable smell of burning coming from somewhere within the house.

By this time he was out in the corridor. It was lighter here, for at one end, about thirty feet away from him, a large uncurtained window was flooded with moonlight. Turning towards the window Daniel gasped. Outlined against the glass stood a man.

'Abel?' He shouted out the name. 'What made you come so late?' He laughed, walked towards the window, forcing himself to smile, his legs wearily and unsteadily obeying the command to carry him forwards. 'We'll have to get a candle. Damn Polly. Whenever she's needed she's not here.'

He stopped ten feet short of the window and said, 'Abel?'

But it wasn't Abel. Not Abel's way of standing, and not the obstinate silence that accompanied it.

'Edgar? What do you want with me?'

He retreated, stumbling back down the corridor, and then finally running towards the stairs. Behind him he heard the sound of footsteps along the uncarpeted floorboards. A door banged. He started coughing. Smoke suddenly billowed out into the hallway.

There was a torch in the kitchen. This was a heavy-duty torch, about fifteen inches long, very heavy and covered with a thick rubber shield. It was, apart from its natural function, a reasonable weapon and formed part of the very considerable array of anti-personnel devices which Polly had brought into the house at one time or another. It hung on a hook, the size used for hanging game, just inside the pantry, and he made his way to it by feeling his way along the wall with his right hand. Once he had the torch in his hand and was able to play the beam in front of him he felt more confident and stepped back towards the hallway.

As he lifted the telephone he was relieved to hear the familiar signal. It took Perkins some time to get to the phone and when he answered there were already flames in the dining-room and smoke was funnelling quickly up the main staircase.

'There's a fire,' Daniel told him. 'For God's sake call the fire brigade. And come yourself.'

'I told you about your wiring, Ross,' he bellowed back. 'You'd think even a damn fool would have had the sense to get it looked at after what happened the other week.'

'There's nothing wrong with the wiring. There's someone here, Walter. I need help.' But he doubted that Perkins had heard the last comment because the line had suddenly gone dead.

Daniel looked uncertainly around him, trying to see through the smoke and the darkened interior of the hallway. If he were to make a run for the front door then he knew that he would be safe. The fire brigade would come and the house might even be saved. But

Edgar would still be on the loose. A lunatic. Completely irresponsible. He'd been a damn fool not to have done anything about him when he'd broken into the house for the first time back in April.

'Edgar!' he called out. The smoke carried him out of the hallway, and without thinking he turned and rushed once more for the stairs. At the top of the first flight he heard what sounded like the suppressed rumbling which precedes the arrival of a train, and it was only then that he realised that the entire back of the house was ablaze, that the brief sharp explosions were from the glass cracking in the windows, and that almost certainly the fire would spread to the upper two floors within minutes.

Behind him a door banged. He spun round in time to see a shadow move quietly down the corridor. 'Edgar, you bloody fool! You don't have a chance of getting away with this.'

He followed. In front of him, as if in broad daylight, he saw Edgar facing him. Daniel rubbed his eyes and cursed the smoke. Ridiculous. He was dreaming. And yet Edgar was in the house. He saw him again, this time moving quickly across the corridor and going into a small room. Daniel followed immediately and shut the door on him, then swiftly turned the key in the lock before throwing it out into the corridor. A box-room, he remembered, a smaller version of the bedroom in which the chests and boxes were stored. It wasn't just Rawley that Edgar wanted, Daniel told himself. He'd tried to kill Jenny. Why not him too? Sweat poured down his face. The whole house was shaking. He could feel it move under his feet.

'I've never done anything to you, Edgar,' he shouted through the door. 'I only tried to help.'

There were no windows in the room, he remembered. It had always been an airless and frightening place to him as a child. A room his mother had kept locked, and whose door he himself had run past in an effort to get it behind him as quickly as possible.

'And what did Jenny ever do to you?' he called out again. 'Nothing. You're all just as crazy as each other. All of you.'

Just down the corridor a few feet away from him was an old sofa. Coughing badly he managed to get to it and drag it back to the door. 'I know it was you, Edgar. The other day. Oh, Perkins might go on about the wiring, but I bloody well know there's nothing wrong with the wiring. You think I'm blind or something?' He pushed the sofa across the hallway so that it would be impossible to open the door even if the lock were broken. 'You think I didn't see the tyremarks? I saw them all right. And everything else. The video. I saw that too. What do you think you're going to do? Clean everything up on your own? It's only more filth you're adding to the mess we've already got. Kill. Destroy. That's all you can think of. But what about those of us who want to live? I want to live, and even Jenny Hallowes, that poor bitch, she too wanted to live.'

He laughed and stood back. From inside the room he heard the sound of coughing. The door rattled.

He turned. At the top of the stairs, his mother. He walked towards her unsteadily. Above him the roof started to collapse. His mother walked down the stairs, and he could see even now the energy in her body as she moved quickly in the direction of George Hutchinson standing in the doorway.

'Ross?'

He looked around him and then clung to the banisters.

'Daniel? For Christ's sake where are you?'

A figure was lurching up the stairs towards him. Outside he could hear sirens. Quite suddenly the smoke and the flames were full of people moving rapidly. Again he heard his name being called. He hesitated, then turned and fled back down the corridor.

They pulled him out ten minutes later, his face badly burned on one side and one arm crushed beneath a fallen joist. He lay, face down, inside the small box-room, having apparently broken his way through the door from the corridor outside. Why he'd gone in there he was never able to say, any more than he was forthcoming about why, as soon as he was out of hospital, he spent so long combing the ruins of the building, searching among the brickwork and the charred wood, as if convinced that he would find something that ought to be there, and yet incredibly was not.

Perkins watched him for some time from the church doorway. It was a cold morning, and he was sorry for Julie because he would have liked her to have had a warm summer's day for the wedding. But it wasn't summer, he checked himself. Pulling his coat tighter around him he reflected that things slipped past him more quickly these days. There was less detail, and perhaps less urgency for detail; and somehow, he thought, he didn't seem to mind too much about it, either. That had always worried him at one time, the thought of growing old and losing the control he'd had over figures and the neat way they all fell together. Well, he'd been mistaken about that. About other things too, even Julie's marriage to Ponting. He remembered talking to Daniel earlier on in the year and saying how disappointed he'd been about the divorce. But it didn't really matter now. Daniel Ross had changed. Julie had changed. And he had the evidence of his own body to prove how much, even over the past few months, he himself had changed. It did worry him though that his daughter hadn't invited him to the ceremony. Callous, he'd told himself when it had first become clear that she didn't want him there. Cold-hearted and an opportunist, just like her mother. Perhaps Daniel was right when he'd said that Julie had only done it so that he wouldn't be hurt, knowing well enough that he'd never made the slightest overture to Ponting nor ever shown any inclination to bring him into the family, but the truth was that he wanted to be there. It wasn't right, her ignoring him like that.

He felt the cold in his hands. September was never like this before, he thought. But then in a day or so it would be October. Time was passing quickly. Autumn was already well set in. What she hadn't counted on was Daniel. He grinned at the surprise he'd give her. Ungrateful bitch, not even telling him the date so that he'd had to learn it from others. Yes, Daniel Ross had changed, and these days she wouldn't know him. Come with me, he'd said. Never mind about the invitation. We'll go anyway. Perkins smiled broadly and then slapped his hands hard together. Damn the cold, he thought, then lifted his eyes to where Daniel stood staring at her grave.

It had been a warm day though, when they'd buried Jenny Hallowes. But then summer had been in full swing. A nice, pleasant day, and a good crowd of people too. Relations, most of them, and Arthur Hallowes by the graveside, his face wet with tears like a young child. But it was Daniel who'd struck him most, standing away by the wych gate, as though he didn't want to be seen with the rest of them. He'd been dressed properly for it, wearing a good dark suit and his shoes blacked so that they shone brightly. Difficult to know what he'd been thinking; it had always been difficult to sort out just what he and Jenny Hallowes had been up to. Of course, Perkins told himself, he'd not lied to Daniel about his feelings towards Jenny. He'd always thought her a fast one; small and thin like that, as his mother used to say, and you never know where they're going to be lying down next, nor who with. There was gossip about her too, not that he'd ever started any of it. How she'd strung that husband of hers along for all those years, and then carrying on with all sorts behind his back. Gossip was fast and malicious, of course, and when it spoke of the accident as being something else he tended to dismiss it. Things like that could get out of hand and there was something indecent about it. In Rawley people talked too much, and when families were prominent, like the Rosses or the Hallowes, then they enjoyed it all the more.

Eleven o'clock, the time that Daniel had arranged to meet him. At the church he'd said. Odd to think of Daniel Ross going into business for himself in town. And odder too to think of the great barren emptiness which marked the spot where Rawley had once stood. There was movement at the far end of the cemetery as Daniel moved away from the graveside. Perkins watched him for a few seconds before stepping out to meet him. Daniel's face was sterner these days, though torn and scarred badly on the right side. Yet there was a purposefulness about him that there'd never been before, there in the walk and the set of the body, there too, in a way that Perkins hadn't noticed before, in the artificial claw that had been fixed to his body after the arm had been taken off.

Daniel had determined that Perkins should have a good day, and in fact he too felt a strong inclination to be present at Julie's wedding. It seemed, more than anything else, an appropriate and perhaps final symbol of his break with Rawley. Whether Julie and Charles would be happy together he didn't know, but he was sure that Ponting was capable of enough deception to ensure that Julie felt happy. A sign of maturity, perhaps, or merely the cynicism which came with experience. He didn't know the answer to that. He did know that he himself had never been capable of accepting his own weaknesses, let alone the weaknesses in other people. And for Julie that could only have been intolerable. He'd been too hard on her, too hard on them all, and certainly too hard on himself. How much he had changed he was not really sure, but he did feel that there had been change, and he felt himself capable of even greater change in the future. As for today, he was sympathetic towards Perkins, alone in his house, with his achievements behind him and nothing in the future but certain decay, and pleased for Julie. And, he had to admit, he looked forward to the slight discomfort they might both feel when he and her father walked in to the registry office behind them.

As it happened they were late for the ceremony and arrived in Chelsea just in time to catch them coming out of the door. Julie in a smart grey suit, quietly smiling, somehow much younger than she should have looked, he thought, and Ponting, grim-faced, surprisingly nervous, ushering his bride out on to the street. When Daniel looked around for Perkins it was to see that he'd been able to contain himself no longer and had rushed forward towards his daughter. Seeing him approach Ponting hesitated, then stepped aside as Perkins swept Julie into his arms.

Behind them and to one side Daniel noticed Helga. Both of them together. Helga and Abel. Abel came out first, tall, full of energy. Oblivious of his elder brother he walked forward to the open door of a chauffeur-driven car parked at the kerb. Daniel followed his brother's movements, his eyes not leaving him for a moment. Then, from the doorway, Ponting and Julie, with Perkins dancing around the pair of them like a young cockerel, moving towards the car.

'Daniel?' He turned, hearing Julie's voice, only to find that it was Helga who had called him.

The car pulled away and dimly he thought he heard the sound of Perkins cackling uncontrollably at the kerbside, though whether with laughter or grief he did not know.

Daniel looked once more at Abel as he stood beside Perkins at the side of the road, taking in his thick matted hair and the strong facial characteristics that had belonged to so many of the earlier Rosses. He then turned back to Helga and found himself drawn to the steady power in her face, and the pride she so obviously took in the child she was carrying.

He'd first found out about the child when he'd come out of hospital. Lillian had given him Helga's new address without question and he'd arrived there one morning, to find Helga down on her knees, polishing the floor. Before anything else was even begun he knew very well that he had to meet Helga again, however painful the experience. Whether she would accept him or not he couldn't know, but he knew he had to try. And then, apart from clearing himself with her, he had to find out what she knew about Edgar. His memories of that last night in Rawley never faltered. However many times he tried to tell himself that he'd been mistaken he was unable to convince himself that Edgar hadn't been in the house with him.

The front door had been open and he'd stood there, watching her polishing the wood around the edge of the carpet in the hallway. A street of terraced houses. A summer's day. Quiet, without traffic.

Seeing him standing there, she'd pulled herself to her feet and said, 'Come in, then.'

She studied him unabashedly, staring first at the scars on his face and then at the empty sleeve of his left arm.

'I was wondering when you'd come,' she had said.

'You expected me?'

He'd watched her wipe her hands on the apron, then lift them to her head where she unknotted the scarf she'd tied around her hair. 'Have some tea?' She didn't wait for him to answer but made for the kitchen, and when he didn't follow called out for him to do so.

The change in her had staggered him. It was not merely the sudden confidence, but the way in which she seemed much older and more commanding. It made him defensive and uncertain of what he was doing there.

Eventually he had asked after Abel.

'He went to see you that night,' she said. 'Said he'd left a message.'

'And I waited. But he didn't come.'

She poured the water into the teapot. 'No. He got scared.'

He thought about that for a moment. It came to him as a shock that Abel was capable of fear. 'What of? Me?'

She laughed aloud. 'Good God, no. Himself.' She tossed her head in an effort to put her hair in place, then whipped her hand up quickly to order a strand that clung obstinately to her forehead. 'Isn't that what it's all about? You. Me. All of us.' Noticing him staring at her, she said, 'You look as though you'd seen a ghost. Sit down, you're making me nervous.'

'What do you mean by frightened of himself?' he asked.

She poured the tea steadily. 'Just that.' She pushed a cup towards him. 'Help yourself to milk and sugar. That's always the way it was. And me too. Scared to help myself. All of us letting ourselves get kicked around.' She cleared her throat, then said, for the first time showing signs of emotion, 'Abel was frightened by that first baby; frightened when it was born and frightened when it died. And that's the way it was with me too. Now it's different. Abel knows what he wants, and so do I.'

Unnerved, Daniel tried to equate this person with the same

girl he'd known earlier. But he couldn't; he didn't know where to begin.

'I wanted to talk about that night I came round to your place,' he said quickly.

'No.' Her voice was flat.

'Please. I can't pretend that it didn't happen, and nor can you.'

'I don't want to talk about it and I don't want to hear you talk about it. What good would it do? If you're worried by what I think of you then forget it.'

'This is wrong,' he protested. 'It shouldn't be like this.'

'Then what do you want?' she asked impatiently.

He didn't know. Forgiveness? Yes. Perhaps the certainty of knowing that what he'd done was wrong, and the certainty too that he was capable of being forgiven. But to know nothing, to live forever in a moral vacuum – no, he couldn't accept that.

'It was my fault. I made you drunk,' he said.

She looked away. 'Yes, you did. I hated you for it. Oh, for Christ's sake, don't push me!'

He felt the barrier rising between them, and knew that she would go no further.

She cried, and didn't flinch when he touched her briefly.

Later, she dried her eyes and fussed unashamedly over her makeup with the aid of a pocket mirror.

'And Edgar?' he had asked at last.

Her face clouded. 'I don't know. I don't know where he is. He left, without saying anything, after the accident. Jenny's accident.' She looked at him squarely and said with firmness, 'I know he did it. I found out about the film. Jenny was always scared to death of him.' She paused, then said, 'Edgar scared us all. Me. Abel. And because Abel didn't know what to do with him or do about him he tried to forget; drinking, drugs, anything he could lay his hands on.'

'Perhaps,' Daniel said, 'perhaps we're all wrong about Edgar. It's possible that he never did anything at all.'

Helga brought down a tin of biscuits from the shelves. 'You know what you are? A dreamer. One of those romantics who by rights shouldn't be around any more. This is planet Earth in the nineteen seventies, Daniel, and people like Edgar exist. How much more proof do you need? He's not here, maybe, but he's out there waiting and one day he'll do the same kind of thing all over again, except it'll be more important and much bloodier.'

Before he left, Daniel asked her something that had been at the back of his mind a long time. 'What does Abel say about me?'

'Not very much.'

'Are you living with him?'

She nodded, then added the single word, 'Yes.'

He stared at her, and it was only then that he was struck by the fullness of her figure. She noticed him and turned away.

'You're going to have another child,' he said.

She faced him. 'Yes. Yes, I am.'

'Is it mine?'

Her eyes did not leave his for a moment, and it was a long time before her face was broken by a light smile.

'Is it?' he insisted.

Now, as they stood together on the pavement outside the registry office, he reflected that the question had never been answered, and never would be.

'I wondered if you'd come,' Helga said, finishing at what seemed some great interval what she had started to say only a few seconds before.

Daniel smiled at her, noticing again the enormous reserves of strength suggested by the way she carried herself.

'What are you going to do now?' she asked.

With his good arm he pointed to Walter Perkins and said, 'Take Walter home. He wants to celebrate a marriage.'

The word set off a chain reaction of images that settled finally on the first occasion when he had returned to Rawley after the fire, and how he had stood at the driveway staring in awe at the immense emptiness that stretched across the fields. The broken walls of the house seemed suddenly insignificant in the enormity of the space behind, and after a time he no longer saw them; it was as if they had been completely swallowed up. It had been a day in July, and the sky had been cloudless, but he had never seen a cloudless day that reached such distances, for there, unmistakably, stretching in a long low line across the horizon beyond the burnt-out house, lay the Downs.

The sound of laughter brought him back suddenly to the immediate present. Walter, with his scant hair awry, and his tie flapping out of his jacket; Helga, with one hand to her hair, and the other pointing towards the road; and Abel, coming slowly into his vision from the right, turning, and saying, 'Daniel.'